EAST COAST MATCHES: BOOK ONE

First Serves and Second Chances

EMMERY FOX

AUTHOR'S NOTE

This story takes place at a fictionalized version of a real college. All tennis results/matches etc are fictional. All members of staff including professors and coaches are also fictional. The fraternities and sororities mentioned are completely made up. While a lot of effort has gone into researching this story, some liberties have been taken with schedules/courses etc for story purposes.

This book is a little angstier than my usual books, so please turn the page for trigger/content warnings. Or feel free to contact me on Instagram @emmeryfoxauthor for more details. HEA promised as always!

TRIGGER/CONTENT WARNINGS

- Death of a parent (past/off page)
- Terminal illness (parent/flashbacks)
- Grief
- Homophobia (no slurs)
- Violence (on page)
- Graphic sex scenes (consensual, safe, vanilla)
- Drug use (mild, on page)

1

NATHAN

My skin prickles, beads of sweat trickling down the neck of my polo. Sun floods the courts, bathing the artificial blue surface in a sickly light. I adjust my cap so the peak's shielding the back of my neck and get ready to return Priestley's serve.

You can get a decent read on some players. Especially if you practice with them frequently. They have tells. The slightest glance to one part of the court. The miniscule turn of a foot.

But Priestley? *Yeah, good luck getting a read on him.*

His body gives nothing away. I watch his eyes over the net, trying to gage where he's looking. *Nada.*

Blood rushes in my ears at the ball toss. His feet leave the court as he brings the racket down. There's that *thwack* as it connects. Priestley's grunt. A split second to react.

I guess left. I'm wrong. The ball flies past me.

When I glance over the net, Priestley's wearing that shit-eating grin I'm sure he came out of the womb wearing.

"Better luck next time, Carter," he shouts across the court.

. . .

By the time we finish practice, my polo's so drenched with sweat, I could wring it out. Priestley's sweating, but not like a pig, not like me. His sweat's almost artful. A few beads on his top lip and dappling the back of his neck under the backward cap.

"Good game," he says as we shake hands over the net.

"Yeah, I'll get you next time."

He laughs, throwing his head back and exposing a long, smooth neck.

"I'm just glad you're on my side," I say.

Kissing his ass feels better than being a sore loser. And we're a team here. If Priestley wins, we all win.

He takes his shirt off, exposing the lean muscles of his perfect, tan skin. I look away, heading over to get some water.

When I check my phone, there's a ton of missed calls, voicemails and messages from my mom, telling me to call her back. *What the fuck?*

I step away from Priestley to make the call. He may look like he isn't paying attention, but I know from experience that he's always taking notes.

"Hey Mom, what's up? Is everyone okay?"

There's a split second where every possible scenario runs through my head. I force myself not to panic.

"Everyone's fine." Mom says.

"So what's wrong? Why have you been blowing my phone up?"

She laughs. "Nathan! I was not *blowing your phone up*. Seriously, sometimes you speak to me like I'm some sorority girl you picked up at a party...."

When she gets worked up like that, her accent comes out —her real one.

"Sorry. You just worried me is all."

She collects herself and takes a deep breath before continuing. "I was calling to let you know that Joe Flannigan died."

The sheen of sweat covering every inch of my body turns suddenly cold. *Shit, I'm not prepared for this right now.* Priestley's watching me discreetly as he sips his water. I realize I haven't responded to Mom and try to find the right words to say.

"Nathan, are you still there?"

"Yeah, yeah, sorry, it's just ... I'm in shock."

"Shock? Nathan, Joe's been sick since you were a kid. You had to know this was coming at some point?"

"I know, it's just ... I don't know." I run a hand over my face, painfully aware of Priestley's eyes on me. "It kind of started to feel like it'd never happen."

A little sigh escapes before she speaks. "I know. But it was no kind of life-"

"When's the funeral?" I cut her off. I want her to stop talking now. Don't want to think about Joe Flannigan in that hospital bed.

"Next Friday. You don't have to come if you have class."

"I'll make it. I should be there."

"Okay. We'll go together. I haven't seen Theresa in a long time, but...." she trails off. I get the feeling she's mostly talking to herself now. Making plans in her head.

"Mom?"

"Yes?"

"Was Evan there? When it happened?"

My face floods the second I say his name. My skin tingling.

There's a hardness to her voice when she speaks again. "Nathan, I don't want you getting involved with that boy again. You know what happened last time."

My stomach clenches. I have to bite my tongue to stop myself from reminding her who's fault that really was.

"I know, I just ... I just wanted to know. I'm not going to get involved with him."

"Promise me."

I take a deep breath and promise her.

She sighs. Her nails tapping on the keys of her laptop. "It says he died at home peacefully, surrounded by his family." She starts reading straight from the obituary and I imagine her at that waterfall island counter she saw from Hillary Duff's house on *AD Open Door* and *had* to have. Tapping her acrylic nails on the granite worktop while she reads about a man's death on her rose gold MacBook Pro. I stop listening until she says Evan's name. " ... son Evan and daughter Stacie."

"Say that part again."

She lets out an impatient huff and I imagine her slamming the laptop shut, the look on her face telling me she's done with this nonsense now.

"Nathan, are you okay? I didn't think this would hit you so hard. You haven't seen Joe Flannigan for years."

A twinge of guilt surfaces, because that's not exactly true. More lies. "I know. I'm fine. I just ... I guess...." *It brought back memories.* "Nothing. It's been a long morning."

"You know ... " There's a long pause and I imagine her biting her lip, grasping for the right words to say. " ... at least he's at peace now."

"I'd better get to class Mom. I'll see you next week."

Priestley's on me as soon as I hang up the phone.

"Has something happened?"

I focus on putting my racket back in my bag so I don't have to look directly at him. "The father of an old friend passed away."

"Oh, I'm sorry for your loss." He pats me on the shoulder with that practiced sincerity people of his breeding are taught from a young age.

"Thanks."

Barely a beat passes before he adds, "You're not going to miss any tennis are you?"

"No matches," I assure him. "But I need to go to the funeral next Friday."

"What about practice? And class?"

"I'll speak to Coach Sanchez, and my professors. I'm sure they'll understand." Translation—it's not your call to make.

He nods, but I can tell he doesn't understand. I'm not even sure *I* understand. Joe Flannigan was not *my* father. But he sure as hell was there for me more than my own dad was.

"We're coming up to the start of the Ivy. It's not ideal to be missing practice at a time like this. We have responsibilities. Sometimes people in our positions have to make sacrifices."

I nod before walking away, letting him know I heard him. But I don't have the mental energy to placate him more than that.

I CAN'T FOCUS during class and I'm still zoned out at lunch. It's only when I'm standing in line at the cafeteria and someone taps me on the shoulder that I remember where I am.

Mira's staring up at me with her big brown eyes, not a strand of her gorgeous black bangs out of place. Somehow she looks perfect despite the fact she's just come straight from tennis practice, too.

"Hey, how are you?"

I want to tell her she can stop this charade of having to say hi and ask me how I am every time we bump into each other. It's been nearly a year since she broke up with me, I'm not mad at her, not anymore.

"I'm fine, how are you?"

She frowns. "You don't look fine, are you sure? Do you need to talk?"

I feel like screaming, *God, Mira, why do you have to be so nice?* It would be so much easier if she was an asshole to me. Then maybe my mom would stop asking about her every time I go home.

"I'm okay." I run a hand over my face. "Just tired."

She cocks her head and keeps her focus firmly on me, and I know she isn't going to let me off the hook that easily. I sigh.

"I found out someone back home passed away."

She grabs my arm. "Oh my god, Nate, I'm so sorry. Who was it?"

I shuffle forward with my tray as the line moves. "You remember I told you about that guy who was dying when I was in school?"

"I think so. The father of an old friend of yours, right?"

"That's the one."

Mira swallows. I try not to watch her as she searches for the right thing to say. She clears her throat before she speaks again. "I'm sorry," she says, the hand on my arm giving a squeeze. "At least he's at peace now."

"That's what my mom said." I flinch from her touch and try to ignore the look of hurt on her face.

"Well, it's true," she says, her voice quiet.

I shuffle forward in the line again and Mira follows me.

"People are going to think you're cutting," I say.

She glances behind her, brushing off the side-eyes she's getting from a couple of girls.

"If you ever need to talk, I'm here for you. You know that, right? Just because we're not dating anymore-"

"I know." I say it a little sharper than I'd meant and she flinches again. "Thank you," I add. "I appreciate it."

I GET my food and take a seat with the guys from the team. Mira takes the seat on Mark's left and he kisses her as she sits down. I look away.

Priestley clears his throat. "Nathan, you'll be at the party tonight?"

It's like one of those questions with only one answer my stepdad is always asking me. The instinct to say, "Yes, sir" pops up before I push it down again.

"Uh, yeah, 'course."

"Good man." He slaps me on the shoulder.

"If you don't feel up to it ... " Mira starts.

I bite my lip to stop myself from telling her to mind her own business. She stopped having to look out for me when she dumped me for someone I thought was a friend.

"Why? What's happened?" Ben asks. He looks so sincere, I can't be mad at him for asking.

"Nothing. Just the father of an old friend died." I'm getting so sick of saying it. But maybe it'll lose its bite the more I do?

"Oh my god, man, I'm so sorry."

Ben puts his hand on my arm and gives it a little squeeze. Little pink blotches appear on his cheeks and he lets it drop.

"Thanks, but it's fine, honestly. He'd been sick for a long time."

"Exactly," Priestley says. "Everyone stop babying him."

I AM NOT ready for this party tonight. I take a quick nap and shower to try and give myself an energy boost.

Maybe I can get drunk and forget that entire phone call with my mom? But, even if I do, when I wake up tomorrow, it'll still be the same. There's only so long you can stick your head in the sand before something bites your ass. I'm pretty sure Joe Flannigan taught me that saying, though I could be wrongly attributing it to him now because he's on my mind.

He taught me a lot of things, though. Like how to change a bike wheel and the oil in your car. Before he got sick, Joe was a normal guy, going to work, spending time with his family, going to the bar occasionally with the guys and getting drunk. Then he got sick and we watched him turn into a shadow. He stopped leaving the house and got hooked up to a respirator. Had a lung removed. Was in and out of the hospital for a while until they realized there was nothing more they could do for him and he chose to receive hospice at home.

I've tried not to think about what Evan was like during all this. We'd stopped hanging out shortly after my mom met Bryce. And before that, we were so young. I doubt I had the emotional maturity to even understand how Evan might have been feeling.

PEOPLE ARE ALREADY DRINKING when I come downstairs.

Priestley spots me walking past the living room and puts his arm around my shoulders, leading me into the kitchen.

"Listen, if you're not feeling up to tonight-"

I cut him off. "I'm fine."

"Good." He gives my shoulder a squeeze. "Because I really need my VP at these things. People expect to see our faces at events, it's part of our roles as leaders of this fraternity."

"I know. Don't worry, I'm here, and I'm fine."

"Good." He gives my shoulder another squeeze before letting me go. "Have a drink, we're going to have some fun tonight."

'Fun' isn't exactly the word I'd choose to describe a forced party when you're feeling like shit, but I can pretend. It isn't like I haven't been practicing for years.

I GRAB A DRINK, just so I have something to hold, and paint on a fake smile for all the people Priestley introduces me to.

As soon as I can, I find a place to hide, slipping into the utility room on the ground floor and find Ben doing the same thing.

"You avoiding everyone too?"

Ben jumps at the sound of my voice. His wide eyes relax when he sees it's only me.

"Man, you scared me! I thought it was Priestley come to chew me out."

"Don't worry about him," I say. But Ben doesn't look convinced.

"Why are you hiding out in here?"

"Why are *you*, Mr. Vice President?" He grins before a blush spreads over his cheeks and he lowers his eyes.

I take a sip of my watery beer and wince. "I'm just not really in the mood for a party tonight, you know?"

Ben shakes his head. "I get it. Priestley should have never made you come. Bereavement leave is something you're entitled to, regardless of what type of job you're doing."

"He's right, though. I have responsibilities. I'll just have to suck it up." Hearing the words, I feel a pang of guilt. My vice president instincts kick in and I say, "Anyway, Priestley isn't so bad."

"Maybe not to you. But he treats me like I'm an idiot." Ben drops his gaze into his cup.

My heart sinks.

"Hey man, don't let him boss you around. He might be the president of the fraternity, but he's not your dad."

This only seems to depress him more. I slap him on the back. "Everything okay? I could talk to him for you, if you want?"

He smiles, and there he is—my carefree friend who always seems to let everything slide off his back. "Everything's fine. Don't talk to him, it'd only make things worse."

I lean against the washing machine, catching the smell of detergent and damp clothes, and make a mental note to find some way to get Priestley off Ben's back without making it obvious. Right now though, I think he'd prefer it if I changed the subject. "So ... see any girls out there you like?"

Ben blushes and rubs the back of his neck. "No, you?"

I hadn't even been looking. I shake my head.

"Have you ... dated anyone, since Mira?"

The cup I raise to my lips swallows my groan. Ben perches beside me, the smell of his expensive cologne mingling with the damp in the air.

"You need to move on," he says. His eyes are planted on the floor.

"It's fine. I'm not even hung up on her anymore."

Ben raises an eyebrow.

"I'm not, I swear."

"So why aren't you out there talking to any cute sorority girls?"

"Can I be honest?"

Ben nods vigorously, giving me that look he gets in his eyes when he's been handed a difficult task and is determined to do a good job.

"The thought of flirting with sorority girls makes me tired."

He's quiet and I swallow, waiting for him to call me weird. But then he bursts out laughing and I'm reminded of why we're friends—and why I'm hiding in the utility room with him instead of partying out there with everybody. Ben and I rushed together freshman year, and there were times when he was the only thing that got me through it all. Any time I tried to talk to my stepdad about how hard it was, he'd just laugh and say, "Welcome to the Ivy League, Nathan." Not helpful.

"I know what you mean. Those sorority girls are high maintenance."

"High maintenance? Mira told me they have detailed checklists for what they're looking for in husbands, and none of us tick off even half their lists."

Ben shakes his head. "It makes sense, I guess. They don't want to end up with a dud."

"Yeah, but this is college. Husbands? Really?"

He laughs, shrugging. "Maybe they're the smart ones? While we're fooling around at frat parties, they're planning their whole futures."

I lean into the washing machine with a sigh. "I guess, but I can't even imagine getting married, can you?"

When I look at Ben, he's gone bright red. He shakes his head.

"What the hell is going on in here?"

We both shoot up at the sound of Priestley's voice. He stands in the doorway with his arms crossed. Shiny, black hair slicked back from his handsome face. He's still wearing the navy blazer he was wearing earlier. He hasn't even undone a button on his shirt. And he'll still look just as polished when the party's over. He looks us both over with disapproval. We look embarrassingly shabby next to him—I'm not even wearing a jacket—but anyone would look disheveled next to Priestley.

"I'd expect this of you, Benjamin ... " Ben and I share a look. No one calls Ben 'Benjamin'. "But my VP? *Come on*."

"Sorry, Priestley," Ben says.

"Don't apologize, just get back out there and mingle."

I slide past Priestley, avoiding his glare as he stands in the doorway, practically blocking my escape. Most of the guys are leaning against walls, flirting with the sorority girls Priestley invited. I hardly ever see Priestley talking to girls at parties. I bet he has one of those 'husband' lists, but for girls. A long, very detailed list of qualities he's looking for in a future wife. I wonder if any woman will ever tick them all off?

I slip into the kitchen before Priestley can grab me and introduce me to the heiress of a diamond mine or something. I'm about to make sure Priestley didn't corner Ben when he slips into the kitchen and stuffs his hand into a bag of chips.

Archer slaps him on the back. "Where have you been?"

Ben and I share a glance. "Just talking to some people," I lie.

Even though these guys are my brothers and we pledged

to look out for each other, I don't want to admit to them all that I've been hiding from the party. Ben is different—I can trust him completely to keep things between us.

Archer slides a Solo cup across the counter to me. I frown, eying it.

"What's in it?"

"Vodka."

I pick up the cup, considering. I shouldn't be drinking vodka at any of these mixers. A couple of beers to look social, as Priestley always reminds me. Nothing more. I'm a leader in this fraternity, I can't be seen getting sloppy and drunk. Plus, Coach Sanchez has us on a strict nutrition plan.

Just as I've decided to decline, citing an early morning workout, Mira comes in from the garden with a couple of friends. She smiles at Mark and then her gaze finds me and turns guilty.

I take the drink and swig it, Archer and Miles cheering me on.

THE NEXT THING I KNOW, we're all chanting *chug, chug, chug* while Miles does a row of shots off the counter. Tears of laughter are streaming down my face by the time he gets to the last one.

Everyone is congratulating Miles for his feat when I spot Priestley making his way through the people mingling in the main room. I grab Ben by the arm, ushering the guys out of the kitchen before Priestley can reach us.

We slip out the back door, all snickering like schoolboys hiding from our moms. A slight chill in the air bites at our exposed arms and faces as we make our way across the soggy grass to the clubhouse in the garden.

The dilapidating shack stinks of weed and sweaty socks, but it's away from Priestley and that's the main thing.

I lean against the wall and sip my vodka while the guys talk about girls.

What would Evan make of this scene? A bunch of frat boys getting drunk, talking about sorority girls. Ever since Mom called to let me know Joe had died, thoughts of Evan have been creeping in every now and then. Just when I thought I'd expelled him for good. Would we still be friends if I hadn't fucked up so badly back then? Listening to Archer lament on the many great (physical) qualities of Zeta Tau president Annabeth Montgomery, a finger of doubt creeps in. It wasn't just that I fucked up, was it? There was the fact that every time I looked at Evan, heat crept up my neck and my pants got uncomfortably tight. No other guy has ever had that effect on me. And that's why I decided Evan was something better kept in the past. But do I still feel that way now? Would he still have that effect on me as an adult? Now I've had an actual girlfriend and I know I'm into women?

"Won't Priestley come in here and find us?" Miles asks as Archer downs the last of his drink. He rolls off his beanbag and starts raiding the mini fridge for a beer.

"No, he hates this place," he says, finding a Coors behind some moldy cheese. "He's been trying to get it torn down since he became president." Archer cracks the beer open and takes a loud swig. "At least when Nathan's president, we won't have to worry about that."

I'm glad it's dark in here so no one can see how uncomfortable I am.

"Why did you guys vote for him?" Miles asks.

"He's not that bad." Archer shrugs, a grin spreading across his face. "Plus, his dad's richer than God and he likes doing all the shit no one else wants to do." He looks at me.

"Your dad's probably the only person who can match the Rosenthal family money."

"He's not my dad," I say, my voice coming out smaller than I'd intended.

Archer just shrugs as he takes a joint from the pocket of his chinos and lights up. "Stepdad, same thing."

Say something, anything.

"I don't even know if I'm going to go for president next year," I say finally, my voice sounding stronger than it did a second ago. "I like being the VP. I'd probably be terrible at it, anyway." Plus, I have way too much on my plate already.

"No, you wouldn't," Ben says.

"All those meetings and organizing everything...." I trail off.

Ben shakes his head. "That's not the only thing the president does. He gets to choose the causes we support and the kinds of things we do for fundraisers. I'm sure you could do better than benefit dinners at the country club for obscure charities no one's ever heard of."

"All charities are good causes," I argue weakly. "Anyway, Priestley *is* our president and I'm his VP, so we shouldn't be talking about this."

"Are you going to tell Priestley?" Archer asks with a raised eyebrow.

"No."

His lips quirk, his eyes saying *I knew you wouldn't.*

The guys fall back into easy conversation, but I'm rattled. I wait until enough time has passed to leave without looking suspicious before going back to the house and sneaking up to my room.

The party is winding down, but the murmur of voices and the soft thump of bass from the speakers still travels through the floor. I try to tune into it, but every time I close my eyes, I see Joe Flannigan in his blue overalls, taking Evan and I out on our bikes. Scolding us for stealing his cigarettes with a sly smile that told us he wasn't really mad. Evan's mom—Theresa—in her grocery store uniform, making us pancakes at the counter before school. That whole world usually feels like a dream. But right now, it's so clear I could swear when I open my eyes I'll find myself in my old room. Evan curled up beside me in an old hoodie. The PlayStation on pause and the light from the TV illuminating his face in a soft blue glow.

2

EVAN

I lie in bed, listening to the sounds downstairs. People have been showing up with casseroles and other shit for days. You can't even get to the kitchen sink for all the bowls and dishes covered in cellophane.

There's a knock on the door and I cover my head with the blanket.

Stacie's voice comes through the wood, quiet and uncertain. "Evan?"

"What?"

"Can I get in?"

I bristle. "No, go away."

She hesitates. As soon as I hear her footsteps on the creaky floorboard, turning back down the hall, I pull the blanket off my head. "*Alright.*"

She opens the door, padding over to the bed in her bare feet. I pull the covers back for her to get in.

She takes up more space that I thought she would. Her cold feet touching my bare calves. When did she get so tall? It feels like I've been asleep for a long time and now I've opened my eyes and the world around me has shifted while I wasn't looking.

She lies on her back, looking up at my ceiling. The tack marks from when I had glow in the dark stars are still up there. Her eyes fill with tears and I clench my jaw.

"You gotta be brave," I say. An uncomfortable feeling in my chest tells me I'm not doing the right thing, that I should let her cry and hug her. But I can't. If I do, I might break down and I can't let myself break down.

The muscle in her cheek tenses as she tries to hold back the tears.

I think about telling her, *It's what Daddy would have wanted,* but I can't even form the fucking words.

Stacie wipes her eyes and I tell myself, *If she can suck it up, so can I.*

I make her get up before Ma can come and ask to get in with us. I don't think I can handle her crying in my bed, too.

Ma's sitting at the kitchen table, dressed, but without makeup on and her hair uncombed. There's something about that half-done thing that makes it worse than if she'd been sitting there in her housecoat and slippers. It's like everything's been turned on its head. Things are kind of right, but not really. And it's that tiny 'not really' that stands out like a sore thumb.

I caught her making the sheets on the bed in the living room before she went to sleep last night and when I asked her why she was doing it, she just pretended she hadn't heard me.

I keep my back to the living room now while I crack some eggs into a bowl to make an omelet for Stacie before she can break into the Pop-Tarts.

More visitors show up. They make a fuss over Stacie.

Gloria from number 28 brings her a fucking Barbie, like she's a third grader. Mrs. O'Conner from next door sits with Ma and tries to get her to eat something.

I manage to slip out when no one's looking. The weight of that house shucks off my shoulders the further away I get.

But the closer I get to the boardwalk, the more a new weight hits me. The guys are all there—leaning against a wall and whistling at the girls as they walk past. At least I managed to get them to stop doing that fucking cat-calling thing after we caught some asshole doing it to my thirteen-year old sister and I broke my hand on his face.

"Hey man, sorry about your dad." Adam says. He slaps me on the back, and for an uncomfortable moment, I think he's gonna hug me. He doesn't, *thank fuck.*

"Forget about it," I say. "He's been dying for ages." I force a hint of nonchalance into my voice that I hope they'll believe. "You wanna score or what?"

Their relief is so visible, I almost laugh. They're so grateful to me for letting them off the hook, for giving them what they want, they follow me like I'm their leader.

We go and score some weed from the guy I know. I've been avoiding him these past few days, knowing he'll want me to move some shit for him. I know the guys'll help me. But they'll want to smoke some, too.

I need the money, but I haven't been able to face the prospect of dealing since those final days of Dad's illness. Well, now I have a fucking funeral to pay for. When someone knows they're dying, they do their best to make arrangements. But in the years since my dad started putting money away for us, the cost of everything has shot up and that money didn't even cover the cost of his treatment. I was lucky the funeral home even let us have a payment plan after all the loans we had to take out when we couldn't pay for years of cancer treatment and at-home hospice care. And those payments are on top of regular utility bills, grocery bills—everything. Mom's salary from the grocery store and my warehouse money just don't cut it.

As I'm leaving, the weed guy calls me back.

"If your ma needs anything, you let me know."

I nod. He's the last person I'd ever ask for help. Nothing comes for free with guys like that. I hide the weed he wants me to sell in the back of my pants before going back to join the guys.

WE GET high in the woods and then go down to the boardwalk when it gets dark. That's when groups of girls come out in short shorts and tank tops, drinking vodka from Coke bottles and smelling of cherry lip-gloss and candy-scented perfume.

The music from the carousel still sounds like someone's winding up a jack-in-the-box too slowly as we weave through groups of tourists and candy-cotton-eating kids. A little boy tugs on his dad's hand and points at the monster trucks and I think about the last time I was on them with my dad. Before I got too cool to hang out with my dad and started coming here with Nate. And now these guys.

For a while, all the guys wanted to do was get laid. We'd take girls behind the fun house, two at a time, so close I could hear Adam's breath right next to me. His cock pumping in and out of whatever girl he was with. His skin slapping against hers and his grunts as he started to get close to coming. I'd try not to think about how much easier it was to stay hard when I tuned into another guy's voice.

Another guy's breath. Back when I was still pretending, even to myself.

They've been more into getting as high as possible these days to make girls a priority. And now we can sneak into clubs, we don't need to get our asses cold doing it outside.

The guys get talking to a group of girls dangling their bare legs over the boardwalk when one of the girl's sandals falls in the water. Adam wades in to get it for her. There's three of them, four of us. If I really wanted, I could beat Paddy to one of them. He's scrawny and awkward as fuck with girls. But I make it easy for them and pretend my ma called and wants me to do something for her. Adam looks like he's going to argue, but then maybe he remembers my dad just died and he lets me go.

I walk back along the boardwalk in the dark with the water a big black mass of nothing beside me and wonder for a second what it would be like to just fall into it. Would it matter? I imagine the water swallowing me up and taking all my thoughts away. Is that what it was like for my dad?

Fuck. No.

I take the long way home. When I get there, my bubbe's holding my ma's hand over the kitchen table. The bed's gone from the living room.

Somehow, the empty space in the middle of the room is worse than the empty bed.

Ma gets up from her seat at the table, wiping her face before she clears away the empty coffee cups and plates full of uneaten food.

Bubbe hugs me. She squeezes me and starts crying. I break free as soon as I can and tell her I'm going upstairs. She looks at me like she can smell the weed, but she isn't gonna say anything while my ma's already upset.

In my room, I put my stash in the old PS2 game case for *GTA: Vice City*. For the first time in ages, I pause at the sight of that game. It's meant nothing to me for a long time—just a place to hide my stash. But now, with everything happening, I look at it like it's the first time I'm seeing it, and memories start rushing over me. Rifling through the dollar bins at *Discount Alley* with Nate. Finding games that were at least ten years old and rediscovering them on my ancient PS2. Getting obsessed with the whole *GTA* series, but this one especially because Nate liked the cheesy 80s music. Driving around, knocking people over. Nate's stupid laugh when that old lady made a weird noise when I hit her with my car. My dad coming home and sitting on the couch in his work clothes and watching us play.

I shake my head to knock out the memory and stuff the case in the back of the bookcase.

Bubbe's heating up one of the casseroles the neighbors brought over when I come downstairs for dinner. She looks me up and down in my work clothes. "Why are you dressed like that?"

"Because I gotta dress like this for work."

Ma's head snaps up from the dishes in the sink. "You're going to work? Evan, call your boss and explain, they're not gonna make you go in tonight."

"I don't wanna call in sick, Ma. I wanna go to work."

They both start talking at the same time until Stacie comes in and tells them to be quiet. Everyone turns and looks at the little girl in her pajamas, eyes ringed red.

"If Evan wants to go to work, you should let him."

Ma sets her jaw and Bubbe looks like she's about to argue again.

"We need the money," I say.

Bubbe shuts her mouth.

"We don't need it that bad," Ma says, but her voice has lost its conviction.

"Yeah, we do."

"Honey." Ma comes closer, running her hand over my shaved head. Back when I let my hair grow, she'd tuck it behind my ear. "You shouldn't have to worry about that. We'll figure it out."

Memories of Dad sitting me down, telling me I'm going to be the man of the house one day and that it'll be my job to take care of Ma and Stacey, surface in my mind. I try to push them down. Because he knew, even then, that this was how it was gonna end. Soon after that, I learned the cancer had spread. Some lady at the grocery store told me and I never said a word to anyone that I knew, just kept it to myself. I straighten my shoulders, look her in the eye.

"It's not a big deal, Ma. It's just a shift, I don't even have to talk to anyone."

She drops her gaze. The nail polish on her thumb is chipped, the spot she bites when she's stressed.

WHEN MY BOSS sees me clocking in, he comes straight over and asks me what I'm doing there.

"I'm down for a shift tonight, right?"

"Yeah, but Evan...." He trails off, rubbing the back of his neck.

I shrug. "I wanna work."

Bob studies me and I force myself to hold his gaze.

"Okay," he says finally. "But if you need to go home at any point-"

"I won't," I cut him off. I don't need babying. "I just wanna work." I repeat. *And we need the money, badly.*

I'm grateful for the monotony of the job. It takes my

mind off things. I make sure not to go on autopilot for once. I leave my earphones out, not wanting to listen to music. Tune into the sounds around me instead. Women complaining about their lazy husbands. The *thump-bump* the machine makes as it churns out more boxes. The *beep* of the forklift truck as someone backs it up.

I don't even realize it's clocking-out time until I look up and see everyone on my line getting ready to leave.

Ma and Stacie are asleep when I get home. The lights all off in the house. I'm careful not to make noise as I come in, walking past the living room quickly to get to the kitchen. Ma usually leaves a sandwich out for me, but this time she must have forgotten. I open the fridge and make my own, eating it standing at the counter. My legs and feet starting to ache now that I'm not focused on a particular task.

It's so dark outside, I can't see shit through the window —just my own reflection as I stuff the last of the sandwich in my mouth. I rinse the plate off, trying not to look at myself.

MA FIXES her tights at the kitchen table while people walk around the house, talking, eating the food people have been leaving for days. Most of it's been taken away again without being touched. Can't say the same about the liquor. I can see how hard they're all trying not to smile. To pretend they don't wanna have a good time.

Ma gets a run in her tights and tries to pull them up so it's hidden under her black dress, but it only makes the run worse. I can't watch her anymore so I get up and go into the garden, walking to the farthest point from the house to light a smoke.

From here, I can watch everyone moving around inside

my house. People we haven't spoken to in years. Everyone wants to be at the funeral of the guy who was dying for years now he's finally croaked.

A familiar face passes by the kitchen window and I have to do a double take to make sure it's really him. Nate Castellani. My next-door neighbor for fifteen years. My childhood best friend. Now he's got his hair in some douchey style and he keeps running his hand through it self-consciously. The suit he's wearing looks expensive, even from all the way out here. A fire burns in the pit of my stomach when I look at his face. It's familiar, like it was the most familiar fucking face in my life for years. Until it wasn't anymore. Seeing how much older he is now, it's like seeing one of those Photoshopped pictures where they've merged a familiar face with someone else's. It's him, but it's also kinda not.

Last time I last saw him, we must have been about eighteen. He was on the boardwalk in his private school uniform with some guys in fancy clothes. I was gonna go over and say hi. A lot of water had passed under the bridge since we'd last seen each other, and to be honest, the sight of his familiar face still drew me automatically to him. But then he looked up, and I swear he saw me. But he looked away, like he hadn't. Like he'd be embarrassed to be seen with me in front of his new, rich friends.

I don't want to think about that stupid day. I'm about to look away when he looks out of the window and his eyes lock on mine. For a second, it's like no time has passed at all. He's still Nate. My Nate. The kid who spray-painted graffiti on the boardwalk because I told him to. The kid I ate Cheetos under the blanket with. Smelling his breath and his sweat and seeing his face so close I could make out the flecks of brown in his green eyes. The guy who's lips I stared at for so long, I could memorize the shape better than my own.

I look away, throwing my smoke into the bushes. Nate, the guy who threw me under the bus when we were fifteen and then left. Pretended he didn't know me when I'd been ready to forget all about that. That guy standing in my ma's kitchen in a designer suit isn't my Nate. *My* Nate doesn't exist anymore. That guy in there is just a frat boy in Nate's skin.

When I turn around, Nate's stepping out of the house and coming toward me. I keep my head down until he's practically on top of me.

"Hey," he says. "Evan, I'm so sorry about your dad."

His voice is different. He talks with some upstate accent now. I bet he calls his ma 'Mom' and his stepdad 'Sir.' I bet he drinks brandy at the country club with his frat bros and those tennis club buddies Ma's always telling me about, like I'd want to know. I wish she'd stop spying on his ma's Facebook page. All people do on social media is brag.

I try to walk around him, but he puts a hand on my chest to stop me. I flinch at the challenge. Finally look up into his eyes. There are those brown flecks, still. That fifteen-year old kid staring out at me through the body of a 20-year-old rich guy.

"Fuck off, Nate."

He frowns, his eyes getting all Bambi-like. A memory surfaces. Nate crying in my bed while he talked about his dad. He hardly ever talked about that loser. The deadbeat left when Nate was five. I didn't even think he remembered him until that day.

I walk around him. I don't wanna look at his sad, familiar-but-not-familiar face anymore.

"Evan."

"What?" I turn around.

He opens his mouth, but nothing comes out. He looks like he changed his mind about what he wanted to say. "If you ever wanna talk...."

"Go back to your frat bros, Nate. You don't belong here anymore."

3

NATHAN

I wish my mom hadn't shown up to the funeral in a Chanel dress with a matching purse and stilettos with bright red soles. I wish I owned a less obviously expensive suit. But I hadn't expected Evan to be so openly hostile.

I know I fucked up when we were kids. I know Evan took the blame, like he always did. But I'd also hoped enough time had passed for him to forgive me. I hoped he'd understand how much I wish I could go back and change what I did that night. Wish I'd done more to protect him, the way he always protected me. I wish I had been braver. But we were kids. So much time has passed. Wasn't our friendship before all that shit important enough to forgive and forget? He ghosted me. It hurt, but I deserved it. I can get through it in light of—what I thought would be—a shared grief. Why can't he?

When I go back into the house, Evan's nowhere to be seen.

Where are his friends? The ones he hung out with at

school? I don't see them anywhere, though I recognize some of the neighbors. Gloria from 28 corners me and asks about college. Old Tom asks me what my plans for the future are. Evan's mom introduces me to Evan's boss. For some reason, I'm surprised Evan has a job. Without realizing it, I guess I'd just automatically assumed he'd be in college, but I guess not. Evan was always the smart one. When we'd sit at that kitchen table right there, doing homework while his mom cooked us SpaghettiOs, I'd copy every word he wrote, until the teacher caught on and blamed Evan for cheating. He still helped me after that, though. Still let me see his answers any time we did one of those multiple choice quizzes.

Evan's house is exactly the same as the house I grew up in before my mom married Bryce. The same tiny, rectangular-shaped kitchen with the table pushed up against the wall. The same narrow hallway and skinny staircase. Same square living room. Three bedrooms—one tiny box room—and a bathroom everyone shares.

I'm pouring myself a soda when Theresa comes and stands beside me. I think she's looking at something out of the window, but when I really look at her, she's just staring into space. She realizes I'm watching and snaps out of it.

"I'm glad you came, Nate," she says, tucking a strand of hair behind my ear. The gesture's way too personal, and yet, it feels natural. "Look at you."

I drop my gaze. I know she's trying to compliment me, so why does it feel like an accusation?

"Your mom's been telling me how well you're doing at college. Your tennis team won a championship or something?"

Inside, I'm cringing, but I force a smile. Her husband just died, and she can retain information like that. And I couldn't even be bothered to come and see him regularly after I left for college? *God I hate myself.*

"Yeah, it was the ECACs last year, we beat Florida in the finals." Why am I still talking? She was probably only being polite and doesn't really give a shit. But she's still smiling. Still paying attention.

Up close, I can see the freckles lining her nose. The grey strands in her dark hair. Evan looks like his dad, with his fairer hair and sharp, unusual features. But he got the freckles from her. She puts a gentle hand on my arm.

"Nate, do you think you could do something for me?"

"Sure." I jump at the chance to make this right. Anything.

"Could you talk to Evan for me? Keep an eye on him?"

I open my mouth to tell her that Evan doesn't seem to want me around, but she interrupts before I can say anything. "I know you're busy at college, but if you could just check in every now and then. A text or a DM. Whatever you kids do these days."

I cover my sigh with a fake smile. Evan made it pretty clear he wasn't interested in talking to me, but I'm not about to stress this woman out on the day of her husband's funeral. "Sure, I'd be happy to."

Her shoulders relax. "You're a good kid, Nate. You were always a good influence on him."

My cheeks flush, because that's not true. Aside from the obvious, we got into trouble on the regular. Shoplifting, graffiti, fighting. But this isn't the time or place to argue.

Mom finds me to tell me she's leaving and asks if I'm coming home with her. I shake my head.

"No, I'm gonna stay for a while."

"Why?" she asks, bristling.

I pull her away from where anyone can hear.

"Because ... Joe was like a dad to me when I was a kid."

She softens a little, but I can see her eyes darting around, looking for Evan. Did she see me trying to talk to him outside? Surely she can understand that I at least need to pay my respects?

"You've said your goodbyes. It's time to move on." She tucks my hair behind my ear and strokes my cheek. The same way Theresa did. Why does it feel so different? How can I tell her, now I'm here, I don't want to move on? That seeing Evan took all the breath from my lungs and I need, somehow, to make it right? It was easy to ignore how hard Evan had it while I wasn't around to witness it. But now I'm here, seeing it with my own eyes, I can't ignore it anymore.

"All the same," I say, working hard to keep my voice level. "I'll make my own way back. There are some things I need to take care of at school anyway."

"Fine." She juts her chin. "I'll see you soon." She looks around at everything like it scares her. "Just don't hang around too long."

I make my way upstairs, a few steps creaking underfoot, and hesitate outside the closed bedroom door I know is Evan's. I listen for a second. There's no noise coming from the other side.

I knock, waiting for a reply. When none comes, I ball my fist up and get ready to try again, but a small voice at my back stops me.

"Nate?"

I turn, blinking at the kid standing in front of me. "Hey Stace, you okay?"

She comes closer and puts her arms around me. She's so big now. The last time I saw her, she was tiny. Hopping across a hopscotch board in the front yard with her friend.

Now she's an actual teenager. Dressed much older, in a stiff black dress and pantyhose.

"You're gonna stay, right?"

"What do you mean?"

"I mean ... " She looks up at me. "You're not gonna leave again, are you?"

Fuck. My heart plummets. I wonder if Evan's listening behind the door.

"Sure."

"I'd leave him be for now," Stacie says, gesturing to the door. "He's less of a grump if you give him space."

"Thanks." I try a smile. "Good to know."

She heads down the stairs and I'm in limbo again, not knowing what the fuck to do. I want to go in there and comfort Evan, but too much time has passed to just jump right back in where we left off. He's made it obvious we can't go back to being friends as easily as all that.

I take Stacie's advice and leave him be. For now.

WE HOST Penn for the first match of the Ivy. Priestley has been on edge for the past 24-hours. Making everyone go to bed early and drink green juice the second we woke up this morning.

While he's off complaining about something, we have a few moments in the locker room to actually have fun. We're laughing and someone's playing music when he gets back. Priestley turns it off, turning to all of us.

"Before you all bitch at me for ruining your fun, I just wanted to remind you all that we're a team out there, and that we've got this."

There's an awkward pause before I realize we're

supposed to cheer. As Priestley's right-hand man, I jump in and start us off, the rest of the guys following suit. Priestley turns to his locker to change and silence spreads over the locker room.

At least the courts look beautiful under the mid-morning sun. There are even a few spectators in the stands. I squint to see if I can find a familiar face, not knowing if I actually want to see my mom there in one of her try-hard designer dresses and her big, bug-eye sunglasses. Instead, I see Bryce, chatting with some serious-looking businessman in a light suit and aviators. Bryce sees me walk out onto the court and raises his hand in greeting.

Princeton is Bryce's alma mater. He got me into competitive tennis after he married my mom, made sure I had access to great coaches. He pulled strings to secure my place. I had to get excellent grades, of course, but I'm not naïve enough to think I'd have ever ended up here without him. Seeing him in the stands makes me even more competitive. Makes me want to show him that his investment paid off.

Priestley and I start play for the doubles point. I didn't particularly want to play doubles with Priestley, I much prefer playing with Ben. But Priestley *is* the better player, and despite how stressful it is being his partner, terrified I'll miss a return or mess up my serve, we win the doubles point and start strong.

Priestley plays the first singles match against Penn's star player. While we watch, I try not to think about Bryce in the stands behind me. We don't get a lot of spectators. College tennis isn't college football or hockey. We're not necessarily a training system for future stars, though there have been pros to come out of the college tennis system. Tennis courts in colleges tend to be crowded together—we're not playing

Centre Court at Wimbledon here. On the plus side, low attendance at matches gets rid of some of that pressure having a live crowd can bring. On the negative side, we'll never get to experience the glory that college football players get to enjoy. And there isn't much of a home crowd advantage, either.

Priestley wipes the floor with Penn's star player and I'm up next.

There's a lot to block out. Not just my nerves at facing an opponent across the net, but Priestley's eyes on me. Bryce up in the stands. The pressure of not letting the team down. And even though I know I shouldn't let the thought distract me, as I step out onto the court, my promise to Evan's mom is running through my mind.

I lose the coin toss, so my opponent serves first. I'm tight, and he serves me two aces. Sweat beading on the back of my neck, I adjust my cap and get into position to await the next serve. This time, I'm looser, ready for it. I return, winning the point.

The match is close, but I win 6-4, 7-5, getting another point for our team.

As I walk off the court, I glance up into the stands. Bryce is clapping, looking pleased with himself before he leans in to say something with a smug expression to the guy beside him.

After we take our showers and change, the guys talk about going out to celebrate, but Priestley warns us about staying fit for the match against Harvard next weekend. The guys groan and roll their eyes when he's not looking, but they get it. We're athletes, and this is important. We need someone like Priestley to ruin our fun sometimes. To keep us on track. Stop our standards from slipping.

Bryce is waiting for me outside the courts, his business associate standing next to him, checking the time on a flashy Rolex.

"Nathan, good match," Bryce says.

The associate shakes my hand and congratulates me on the win.

"Not a Princeton man myself," he says. "I was at Stanford."

I nod, knowing the script by heart.

"Stanford has a great tennis team." Stanford is our closest rival. It rankles a little having to hype it up.

"Excellent," the associate agrees with a nod.

Bryce clears his throat. "Nathan, let me take you for lunch."

I'm about to make up some excuse about a meeting at the frat house or a class I have to rush off to, when Priestley comes jogging over, looking fresh in his crisp polo and chinos, like he hasn't just played hours of competitive tennis.

Bryce lights up at the sight of him and they shake hands like old friends.

Bryce doesn't even have to introduce the associate, Priestley shakes his hand and asks about his wife and kids.

"Priestley, why don't you join us for lunch?" Bryce asks, as if I've already said yes.

"I'd love to, but I have some pressing fraternity matters to take care of."

"That's a shame. You don't mind if I steal Nathan, do you?"

Priestley slaps me on the shoulder. "I'm sure I'll manage without him for a few hours." *Great, thanks.*

Bryce starts talking business the second we sit down in the stuffy bistro. The place is full of businesspeople in stiff suits discussing mergers and stocks over grilled salmon and bloody cuts of steak. Despite taking a shower after the match, I'm worried I smell bad. The armpits in my nice shirt are already wet.

"I was just telling Mason about the little business venture you have going with your friend, Ben," Bryce says, trying to draw me into the conversation.

Mason seems to have that smug grin surgically etched onto his face. He looks over at me, still caressing the stem of a wineglass he's been nursing since we sat down.

"You know John Harris?" Bryce turns to Mason. "Ben is his youngest."

"Ah, of course, John Harris. I saw him last week at the club ... "

I zone out while they talk about old friends and business associates and gossip from the country club. It took a lot of getting used to when I joined private school in my soph-more year of high school. Everyone knowing each other already, people judging you by who your dad is. I quickly learned that it was best to tell them about Bryce rather than say my dad left when I was five. Nothing screams 'trailer trash' quite like not even knowing where your father is. *He's on a six month business trip in Dubai and you can't remember what he looks like? Fine. He walked out on you one day when he was supposed to be buying milk? Low-class.*

Eventually their conversation circles back to my venture with Ben. Mason asks me to describe the concept. Luckily, Ben and I have discussed it so thoroughly, I know the words by heart. I tell Mason how we plan to create a database for players to find not only coaches, but nutritionists, trainers, sports psychologists, and even other players to practice with.

What would make our database different from all the others would be the ability to find everyone in one place and the fact we will branch out into tennis academies one day. Find sponsorships for players from low-income areas. Build courts in these areas and have college tennis players volunteer at schools to get more kids into tennis—not just rich kids whose parents already belong to tennis clubs. Or, like Ben, whose parents actually have a tennis court on their property.

"Your idea sounds solid, Nathan," Mason says. "Do you have a business plan? Have you thought about backers yet?"

My armpits are swimming now. If I'd have known this lunch was going to turn into an episode of *Shark Tank,* I would have prepared more.

I clear my throat, trying to ignore Bryce's gaze.

"We're still in the early stages right now ... " *God am I putting a 'telephone voice' on, like Mom?* "But we should have a more solid business plan by the end of the academic year."

"As you can imagine, Nathan has a lot on his plate in his junior year, what with tennis and fraternity duties," Bryce jumps in, like he's saving me. My hear sinks. Did I do badly? "Being Vice President isn't easy."

"Vice President, really? It's Sigma Alpha Psi, right?" Mason sounds impressed, not surprised. That's good, at least.

I nod while he wipes his mouth on a napkin.

"Why don't you give the office a call once classes are out and we'll have a little chat?" He hands me a business card. One of those fancy types with embossed lettering.

"Thank you, sir, I will."

My hand trembles a little as I put it in my pocket. I didn't realize how quickly I'd have to start acting like an adult when I left for college. How suddenly I'd be thrust into the grown up world of business. But I find myself eager to impress. Keeping the business cards of all the associates Bryce introduces me to in a drawer in my room. Practicing my speeches in the mirror. Learning when to laugh and when to be serious. When to be jovial and when to be cutthroat.

Bryce hangs back after Mason leaves. A hand on the back of my neck guiding me towards his car.

"You did well, Nathan."

My shoulders sag with relief and this ball of warmth emanates from my chest.

"You've come a long way. I keep telling you, it doesn't matter where you start, if anything, starting at the bottom can make you hungrier, deadlier. I wasn't born into money either ... "

I nod while he recounts a favorite tale of hardship before he reached the dizzying heights of CEO. Bryce likes to think he's above men born with a silver spoon in their mouths because he had to claw his way to the top, but personally, I hate being reminded that I wasn't born to live in this world. He can't even imagine how hard it was having a strong Jersey accent in private school, before I learned how to refine it. Bryce's version of 'hardship' is growing up middle-class in Connecticut and having to attend public school before getting a scholarship to Princeton.

"You get back to school and focus on your studies now. Keep your eye on the prize. Don't let anything distract you," he says, giving my neck a final squeeze before letting me go.

THE NEXT MORNING, I slip out of the frat house before anyone is awake. I have a destination in mind, and the closer

I get to it, the more the hairs on the backs of my arms start to bristle.

Joe Flannigan's funeral was the first time I'd returned to this neighborhood in years. It felt weird coming back, seeing my old house next to Evan's. A new car parked in the driveway. Different kids playing out on the lawn.

The house is quiet now as I pull up, the screen door and crumbling porch exactly how I remember.

I park the SUV Mom and Bryce bought me for my 20th birthday at the end of the driveway and hope Evan doesn't take one look at it and tell me to fuck off.

His mom's car isn't parked in its usual spot, so she must have gone back to work already.

As I get out of the car, I try not to think about the last thing he said to me at the funeral. *Go back to your frat bros, Nate. You don't belong here anymore.*

Was he right? I've never felt like I fully belong in Bryce's world. For the past five years, I've been telling myself this disconnect is due to the fact that I belong *here*. But if that isn't true either, what the hell is the issue? Where do I belong then?

Faded chalk marks from Stacie's hopscotch board are still visible on the driveway. The basketball hoop Evan's dad put up over the garage door is still bolted in place, starting to rust. The sight of these familiar touchstones bring up memories that I haven't thought about for years.

When we were kids, I followed Evan around like a puppy dog—jumping into the sea after him, trying to keep up at basketball, helping him steal cigarettes from his dad's overalls and trying to smoke them under the boardwalk. I always thought that felt like a long time ago, but standing here on his doorstep, waiting with sweaty palms for him to come and open the door for me, it feels like no time has passed at all.

Except when Evan comes to the door, he isn't a gangly fifteen-year old anymore. He's a grown-ass man in a ratty white vest and sleep shorts. I swallow, remembering that thing I'd pushed down more than any other memory. How I'd watch Evan smoking one of his dad's Marlboros and think about his lips on the filter when he passed it to me. Hiding my excitement from him when we stripped down to our underwear to jump into the sea. He scowls when he sees me.

"What do you want?"

I swallow, paste on my best smile. "Hey."

"My ma's not home."

"I didn't come here to see her."

"What do you want?" he repeats, a little more exasperated this time.

I shrug. "I thought we could hang out."

He lets out something between a laugh and a scoff. "What's wrong? Your frat bros all busy hazing kids in the basement?"

I'm momentarily stung, but remind myself that he's just angry, and grieving. And he has every right to be angry at me. I got us into trouble back then. I wasn't there for him when he needed me most. But I'm here now. Even if he thinks he doesn't want me to be.

"We're not that kind of fraternity." I say evenly. "And hazing is illegal."

Something flashes in his eyes and I force myself to hold his gaze, hoping he can see the apology behind them.

"Oh yeah?" He crosses his arms and leans against the doorframe. Something flips in my stomach. His pecs in that vest, his biceps. The definition of muscular shoulders. He didn't look like that when we were kids. "So what kind of fraternity are you?"

I know he's clowning me, but I go along with it anyway.

"The kind who does volunteer work at nursing homes and has long, boring meetings."

The smirk falls from his face. He looks me up and down.

"So what are you doin' here, Nate?"

"I told you, I want to-"

"Not the bullshit reason, give me the real one."

I sigh, stuffing my hands in the pockets of my chinos. "Your mom asked me to keep in touch."

"Pshht, I fucking knew it."

He tries to slam the door in my face, but I put my hand on it, wedging my foot between the door and the jamb. I note the surprise on his face at how much stronger I am now.

"Wait. I wanted to come over here, too."

His face is scrunched up into something I don't recognize in him. "Nate, get the fuck out of my way."

"Or what?"

His nostrils flare, and for a second, I actually think he might hit me. The Evan I knew would never, but I'm quickly realizing that this guy standing in front of me isn't my Evan —not the parts I can see, at least.

"Wouldn't it just be easier to let me in?"

The look on his face tells me he's still not convinced.

"Just to set your mom's mind at rest?"

"Pshht," he says again. "Knew it."

"Knew what?" I try a smile, my stomach doing somersaults.

"You'd be saying 'Mom' now. When we were kids, you called her 'Ma.'"

"Pshht," I try, but it sounds weird coming out of my

mouth. If I spoke to my *mom* like that now, she'd have a fit. She'd also have a fit if I called her 'Ma,' though I did for years.

"Yeah well, she's all fancy now. She doesn't like being called Ma."

"*She's* fancy?" He looks me up and down. My Ralph Lauren polo and Abercrombie chinos. Heat floods my entire body as I feel his eyes on me.

"Are you gonna let me in or what? The neighbors will start to talk."

"Nah, they'll just think the Mormons are doing their rounds again."

"What's wrong with Mormons?" I ask, hoping this verbal sparring will distract him from slamming the door in my face.

"You're right. They don't hassle people half as much as you."

I shrug. "I'm not leaving, not until you let me in."

He swallows, the smirk dropping from his face.

"Ma's home in an hour. You can stay till she gets back, show your face, then leave. Obligation over."

I nod, my heart sinking.

He lets out a big sigh before turning and walking into the house, leaving the door open behind him. His bare feet slap on the vinyl on his way to the kitchen.

"You want a drink?" he calls to me. "Something to eat? We've got enough casserole for a year out here."

I follow him out and lean against the counter while he pours two glasses of juice.

"You still drink store-brand, right?"

I pull a face and he almost smiles.

He puts the juice on the counter by the sink, just out of reach.

"Can I have that?"

Ignoring me, he says, "Shouldn't you be playing tennis or throwing a frat party or something?"

"I'm off-duty today."

He rolls his eyes and turns to the window, leaning against the sink and gazing out. The sun coming through the glass highlights the muscles in the backs of his arms.

"I met your boss at the funeral."

He stiffens at the word 'funeral'.

"Where do you work?"

"A warehouse. Why?"

"How long you been working there?"

"Since school."

He pushes off from the sink and looks at me, a challenge in his eyes. "We don't all have rich stepdaddies to pay for Ivy League colleges. Some of us have to contribute."

I flinch, but he's not looking at me to catch it. "I know what you're trying to do, and it's not going to work.

I'm not only here because your mom asked me. When I saw you at ... I realized I should have made more of an effort. I did go and see your dad at the hospital, but you were never there and-"

"You went to see my dad at the hospital?"

"Yeah, of course. Your dad taught me how to ride a bike. He was there more than my own dad was. My real dad."

His face softens and he wraps his arms around himself.

Neither of us have touched our drinks. The silence starts to build.

I know somehow that it's my responsibility to break it, so I say the first thing that comes to mind. "Hey, you still got *GTA*?"

He blinks hard at me, like I'm speaking a foreign language.

"Yeah," he says finally. "The PlayStation's in the living room, Stacie made me move it."

"She *made* you?" I smirk.

"Yeah." His lips quirk the slightest bit. "That's what I said."

"Wanna play?"

He swallows and licks his lips before casting a worried look towards the living room.

"What's wrong?" Did I say something wrong? The realization hits me that the living room is probably where his dad slept, in the end. I start to apologize, but he cuts me off.

"You set it up, I'll go and get the game."

4

EVAN

When Ma comes home, Nate's sitting on the living room couch with a PlayStation pad, driving into people on the sidewalk. She beams when she sees him.

"Nate, hi!"

He hits pause on the game, gets up to help her with the groceries. Must be all those Ivy League manners he's learned. Helping old ladies across the street before feeling up drunk cheerleaders at a frat party.

She tries to wave him away but it doesn't work. "You guys go and play, I'm fine, it's just salad. I needed a palate cleanser after all that casserole, not that I'm not grateful ... "

They're still talking in the kitchen so I turn the game off. I haven't been alone in the living room since they got rid of my dad's bed. I'd forgot about it while Nate was here, distracting me with the stupid game. If I look at that spot, I can see him still, propped up on some pillows, me on the couch, wondering if he's actually watching the TV or just pretending. I turn around and get out of there as fast as I can.

"You wanna stay for dinner, Nate?" Ma asks.

"I'd love to, but I have a meeting at school."

"Meeting? Sounds serious," Ma jokes.

"It's just a fraternity thing."

"Oh, of course."

"Come on, frat boy," I say. "I'll show you out."

"Evan, walk Nate to the bus stop," Ma says.

"It's okay, thanks, I have my car."

"You haven't left your Rolls Royce parked up in this neighborhood, have you?" I make a face and he rolls his eyes.

"Nate, do you drive a Rolls Royce?" Ma asks, eyes wide.

"No Ma, I'm just fucking with him."

"Oh."

He hugs her goodbye. I walk to the end of the driveway with him so I can make fun of whatever flashy-ass car he does have.

"Oh, it's a Beemer, my mistake."

Nate actually blushes. "I didn't ask for it, my mom and Bryce bought it for my birthday."

My ma's beat up Honda sits parked in front of a garage too full of shit to use for cars.

I think about telling him he doesn't need to explain himself to me. If I was rich, I'd be driving a BMW, too. But I don't want to encourage him. Can't have him coming round here any time he likes, in his fancy clothes and his expensive car, dredging up things that don't need dredging up.

"It was good seeing you," he says.

"Yeah." I rub the back of my neck.

I turn around and walk back toward the house as he gets in his car. I need a second before facing my ma and her questions. Her happiness over Nate being here.

Nate just got lucky. Anybody would find it hard to fuck

up if they had an Ivy League education all paid for and enough extracurriculars to distract them from drugs and whatever other vices people get into. And a rich, well-connected stepdad to bail him out of trouble whenever he did fuck up. Like last time.

I take a deep breath before going into the house. Ma's putting the salad away and I help her.

"He's already being a good influence on you."

"Stop it, Ma."

"What?"

"I know you like Nate, but he's not gonna be coming round here often."

She makes a big deal of fluffing a pack of lettuce. "Why not?"

"He's only here as a favor to you and because he feels sorry for me."

She turns with the lettuce. "You don't know that," she says, putting it in the fridge. Under the light, I notice her nose is red and I wonder if she was crying in the car before she came into the house.

"Did you know Nate went to see Dad in the hospital?"

She nods. "He was there a few times, yeah. Why?"

"Why didn't you say something?"

She bristles. "I thought he would have told you himself. I had my mind on other things."

I drop my head. "'Course, sorry."

"He's a nice boy." She sighs. "I'd like you to be friends with him."

"Instead of my friends?"

There's a beat before she answers. "You know what I think of them. They're losers, Ev."

"Maybe I'm a loser?"

She scrunches her face up and I'm sorry I said anything.

"You are not a loser. You have a job, and if you wanted, you could get your GED and go to college. Those idiots don't have two braincells to rub together."

I snort. Ma runs her hand over my shaved head and studies me until I drop my eyes. "You used to have beautiful hair."

"Like pretty boy Nate?" My face gets hot.

I meant to say preppy boy, not pretty boy.

"Not like Nate. Like you."

I go up to my room and flop down on the bed.

Pretty boy Nate. That little slip of the tongue keeps running through my head. How many times did I rub one out over Nate when we were younger? He was always the kind of 'cute' girls would lose their shit over, but he wasn't vain about it. It was like he didn't even notice.

I always told myself my little crush on him when we were kids was due solely to the fact he was the boy I was closest to when I started having thoughts like that. Not because of him. Seeing him today, I'd be lying if I said I wouldn't be into him if I passed him on the street. But I'd never sleep with someone like him. He's too perfect. I don't fuck people who can judge me.

I GET A TEXT FROM ADAM.

Meet me after work.

I know what he wants. I've got a new stash to sell and I need the money, so when I change into my work clothes, I stuff just enough into my steel-toe boot before putting on my Dickies and a polo with the warehouse logo stitched onto the chest. A big coat, too. Even in the summer, it's freezing in the warehouse.

I'd lose my job if Bob caught me with this shit at work. But I need to take the risk. The little side-hustle pays more than my minimum wage packing job, but it's less steady, and I need steadiness too.

One of the perks of shift work is that you miss rush hour. There's hardly anyone on the bus. A couple of teenagers sitting on the backseat listening to shitty electronic music on their iPhones. A woman my ma's age in nurse's scrubs, rubbing her feet and yawning.

I clock in when I get to the warehouse and put my earphones in to go and start packing at the conveyor belt when Bob steps in front of me. I take my earphones out, my music blearing.

"How are you doing, Evan?"

I shrug. "Fine."

"How's your mom?"

"She's fine ... " I remember this guy's my boss and alter my attitude. "Thanks."

He gives me an awkward pat on the arm and I walk around him to get on with my job, but he calls me back. "Oh Evan, I know it's a bad time, but I was just wondering if you'd thought any more about the electrician course?"

"Uh, no, sorry, I haven't really had time-"

He holds his hands up. "No worries. Just let me know when you've decided, I think you'd be great for it."

I turn my music up and try to zone out, but I'm thinking about that stupid course Bob's been trying to get me to go on for months.

Everyone's trying to be like those big companies now, selling the illusion that they're more than a sweatshop paying everyone minimum wage and milking them for their cheap labor while making a CEO rich. No matter what Bob says about me taking the opportunity for free training, I can't see anything this place does as benefitting me. I don't want to roll over and be their lapdog and thank them for the chance.

After the first fifty boxes, I start to get into a rhythm and forget where I am. Some of the women talk while they work, but mostly people just look like fucking zombies, like me, busting their ass doing the same thing over and over until clocking-out time.

I get a break four hours into my shift and pour a strong coffee into a scalding hot plastic cup to keep myself awake, eat a Snickers, and check my phone.

Another text from Adam:

What time do you finish?

He must be desperate.

Eleven.

Meet you there.

I go back to my shift, on edge from the coffee and the thought of having to go out and do more work. Work that could get me into trouble if I got caught.

I clock out, in no rush for once to get out of here.

Adam's there when I get out to the parking lot. He's not alone. Never alone. Corey and Paddy lean on the wall, looking conspicuous as fuck. I briefly consider walking past and not looking back, but I can't do that. I pull the collar of my coat up and hope Bob doesn't see me meeting these guys.

Adam stands up and slaps my hand. I nod. "Hey, man."

He licks his lips. “Shall we smoke some before we go out?”

“I’ve only got enough to sell.”

“We’ll put it back, won’t we?” He turns to Corey and Paddy and they nod.

My heart sinks. These guys aren’t exactly ‘friends’. They don’t know shit about me. I wouldn’t trust them as far as I can throw them. But they’re all I have outside of work and my ma and Stacie. And then there’s the prospect of getting high. Forgetting everything for a while. Taking a vacation from life.

“You’ve gotta put it back, though. I’ve got bills-”

“Don’t worry.” Adam pats my shoulder before looping his arm around my neck. “We won’t let you down. You need to relax man. Doesn’t he need to relax?”

Corey and Paddy nod.

I can barely keep my eyes open when we go down under the boardwalk to smoke. The stress of the day shucking off my shoulders as the weed takes effect. Making me want to curl up and go to sleep.

“Our working boy,” Paddy says, patting me on the back. They all laugh. “You don’t need the job anymore. Why don’t you just quit? It’s not like you have to pay your dad’s med bills anymore-”

“Shut the fuck up, idiot.” Adam clips him on the back of his head.

“Shit. Sorry, man.”

“Forget it.”

It doesn’t bother me, him talking like that. Plus, he’s wrong. Just because we don’t have medical bills to pay doesn’t mean we don’t have bills. Taking loans out was stupid. Loans aren’t medical expenses. But we thought we could pay them. We thought we could avoid bankruptcy.

Living without credit isn't easy when you make minimum wage. I knew we'd need a payment plan for the funeral. I was trying to plan ahead. But we can still pay everything off, if I just try harder. If I stop smoking what I'm supposed to sell.

My ma's in bed when I get home. She's left me a sandwich under a paper towel in the kitchen with a note saying 'eat something before bed.'

I demolish it standing up, still wearing my boots and coat.

5

NATHAN

I've lived in this big fraternity house for years now. I almost stopped looking at it, like really looking at it, until recently. Being back in my old neighborhood makes the smallest things stand out now. Like the fact we have our own library with walls and walls of leather-bound books. Or a chandelier in the entranceway. Things that Priestley Rosenthal wouldn't bat an eye at, but things the child me would have found ridiculous.

After another meeting, I head toward the front door, getting stopped by about five different brothers on my way out. I have to smile and talk to them like I'm not in a rush.

After chipping away at Evan's resolve last time, I made a vow to keep trying to break through with him. The first step was staying up late last night to finish a paper for my economics class so I'd have time to go to his place after our weekly Philanthropy committee meeting.

SECOND STEP IS ACTUALLY GETTING Evan to let me in again.

After I park the car at the bottom of the driveway,

making sure not to block Evan's mom in, I take a deep breath and knock.

Theresa opens the door in her work uniform. She looks so grateful to see me, I feel like the worst person on earth. What would she think if she knew I was the reason Evan and I got arrested back then? That it was my stupid mistake that made him fuck up? That he was only there because I called him to help me clean up my mess? Would she be smiling at me then?

"Come in, Evan's still asleep, but he should be up soon."

"Oh ... I can come back some other time."

She's already turning, heading back into the kitchen. "Come on in, have some coffee. I was just about to put some on before work."

I follow her through the house to the kitchen, still freaked out by how familiar the layout is to my own childhood home.

"How's your mom, Nate?"

She talks with her back to me, filling the old coffee maker they've had forever.

"She's good, thanks."

My stomach flips at the sound of footsteps on the stairs. Evan's probably going to be pissed that I'm in his house. When I turn around, he still looks half asleep in the doorway in a pair of grey sweats with no shirt on. The gold St. Christopher I remember him wearing when we were kids dangling between his collarbones. My mouth waters and I turn away.

"Hey, you're up. Coffee's on," Theresa says. She doesn't seem fazed that he's half dressed. Of course she isn't fazed. She's his mom. She sees him like that all the time. But I haven't seen him without a shirt since we were kids, and he looked a lot different back then.

He rubs his eyes before frowning at me. "What are you doing here?"

"Evan!" Theresa flashes me an apologetic smile.

"I didn't know you'd still be asleep," I explain.

"I worked a late shift last night." He yawns, raising his arms above his head. Something gnaws in the pit of my stomach at the sight of fair hair in his pits. A faint hint of the way he'd smell whenever we curled up and fell asleep together.

"No classes today, Nate?" Theresa asks, obviously trying to get the conversation going.

"No, I had a paper due in today, but I finished it last night."

She nods before taking a sip of her coffee. "What was your paper on?"

"The benefits of humane capitalism ... " My neck burns. I can *feel* Evan judging me from across the table.

Silence falls over the room and I wrack my brain for something to say.

"Where's Stacie?"

Theresa answers. "She's at hockey practice."

"Ice hockey?"

"Yeah," she laughs. "She's a little bruiser, than one."

"You shouldn't let her play, she's gonna get hurt," Evan says.

Theresa rolls her eyes. "Mr. Protective over here."

She takes a few more sips of her coffee and checks her little leather wristwatch.

"Is that the time? I'd better go."

After dumping her coffee cup in the sink, she bends to kiss Evan on the cheek. "See you later, don't make the house a mess."

After the front door bangs closed, Evan and I look at

each other. I offer an awkward smile and he looks down into his mug.

"I've got some shit to do today," he says.

"Oh, okay. I can tag along if you want some company."

There's a split second where his eyes get wide, but he recovers quickly and I know he's hiding something.

"It's work stuff. You can't."

"Oh, okay."

Didn't he just say he did a late shift last night? And Theresa didn't mention anything about him going back into work already. But I'm getting dangerously close to 'mind your own business' territory, so I don't ask.

"Will you be busy later? Maybe we could do something when you're finished with your work stuff?"

He looks intensely into his coffee cup and for a second, I think he isn't going to answer.

"Listen, Nate, you don't have to-"

"I know I don't," I cut him off. "Can you just humor me? Please?"

He shrugs. I take that as the closest thing to a yes I'll get for now.

I write my number down on a legal pad by the phone where his mom or someone has doodled all over it with names and numbers. There's medical-looking stuff on there too, probably about Evan's dad.

I wonder if he's grieved properly yet. If he'd lose his shit if he saw the notes on this pad, or if he's not in that place. I have no idea how to grieve for someone that close to you, I've never even lost a grandparent and I barely remember my dad. As far as I know, he isn't dead. I think I've been grieving for Joe, but it feels wrong, like I'm not allowed to.

I leave Evan to do whatever he has to do. He was probably just trying to get rid of me. I think about leaving him alone. Giving up. I promised his mom I'd try and I tried. If he doesn't want me around, I can't force myself on him. But then I pass that rusty hoop in the front yard and Stacie's hopscotch board and I get a dragging feeling in my chest that is more than just nostalgia. Making me feel like that kid again. The one who worshipped the ground Evan walked on. Who looked at him like he was the fucking sun. Because he was. And because I owe him this much at least.

That night. *Fuck.* I've played it over and over in my head. What I could have done differently—everything. For starters—not stealing a car to impress Evan. Secondly—not calling him when shit hit the fan. Leaving him out of it. I can't change the past. But I can be here now. So that's what I'm going to do.

I WANT to avoid anywhere someone from the frat or tennis team might grab me and take over my evening, so I go back to my mom and Bryce's house to study and get a bit of peace.

They're not usually home during the day. Bryce works crazy CEO hours, and Mom's social calendar is always full, so my heart sinks when I spot Bryce's black Mercedes SUV parked in the driveway. Hopefully the fact he hasn't parked in the three-car garage means he isn't planning on staying long. I might still get the house to myself for a few hours.

He's in the kitchen on his phone when I come in and put my bag down.

"Nathan," he says when he hangs up. "What are you doing home?"

"I just wanted to get some studying done in peace."

I wait for him to ask me if the library isn't peaceful, but to his credit, he doesn't.

"I'm heading out in a few minutes, I just had to pop back for some papers. How's school?"

"Good."

I pick an apple out of the fruit bowl and give it a squeeze to make sure it's real. I've been fooled by my mom's expensive fake fruit before.

"And tennis? You think you'll make it to regionals this year?"

"We've got a good shot."

"Nathan, I want you to really focus on school this year. Mason Mathews doesn't offer just anyone business advice."

"I know that, and thanks. I appreciate you helping me out." My neck heats as he scans me.

"I know tennis is fun, but you're not going to be a professional. Don't let it get in the way of your studies. That's where your future lies."

"I know."

I think he's done with me and am about to excuse myself to go to my room when he speaks again. "And Nathan."

I spin on my heels.

"I understand why you felt the need to attend the funeral of your old friend's father, but your mother's worried you'll be tempted to pick up your communications with him."

My heart sinks. My face flushes. Does he know I've been seeing Evan? Surely he wouldn't have me followed?

"Trust me when I tell you, the circles you'll be running in when you graduate won't tolerate smudges on your reputation. When you leave the fraternity, your brothers will become your competition and the margins of error are tiny. You all have an Ivy League education and you'll all have excellent grades and extracurriculars on your resumés. Don't let a little thing like a bad rep get in the way of putting you ahead."

I just stare at him, trying to think of something to say. What a depressing picture he just painted. My fraternity brothers becoming my competition. So what's the point of building up fraternal spirit with these guys if I'm planning to elbow them out of my way as soon as the opportunity arises?

Thankfully, his phone starts ringing and he turns away from me to answer it.

I TRY TO STUDY, but even after I hear Bryce's car pull out of the driveway, I can't get his words out of my head. *The circles you'll be running in when you graduate won't tolerate smudges on your reputation.*

What if Bryce finds out I'm seeing Evan? Will he tell Mason Mathews not to work with Ben and me on our business idea? I've never openly defied him, so I have no way of knowing how he'd react. If he was angry, how far he'd go to protect his reputation. And this isn't just me we're talking about here. This affects Ben, too.

I think about not texting Evan. It's not like I'm ghosting him—he's made it clear he's only barely tolerating me. But then I think about how much it hurt when he didn't reply to my messages back then. And how it was my fault everything went down the way it did. I think about him working in a warehouse somewhere to pay his bills. How alone he must have felt when his dad was sick and his best friend was nowhere to be seen. And who was there for him after I left? I didn't notice anyone filling my spot. I can try and be there for Evan without fucking things up with Bryce. Bryce doesn't have to know. I take a deep breath, typing the message.

Can you still hang out?

My heart pounds as I wait for a response. Is he going to ghost me like last time? Would I still deserve it now? Finally a message comes through:

My place.

I pack my shit up straight away and head out.

6

EVAN

I manage to move the rest of the weed and pay my guy, having to dip into my own money to cover what we smoked last night after work. I promise myself I won't do that again.

I tell myself I invited Nate over just to get him off my back. But that doesn't make any sense. He's like a fucking boomerang. The more you throw him away, the more he comes straight back. I tell myself I can't remember him being this annoying and persistent when we were younger, but that's a lie. He always was like my shadow, following me around. Sitting on my stoop every morning, waiting for me to come out, until Ma just started leaving the door open for him to walk in and sit at the breakfast table with us while his ma was at work or out with some guy. I know Ma felt sorry for Nate back then, but I didn't. He was my equal. I felt protective over him, but not sorry for him. Now the tables have turned and I can't stand the thought of Nate feeling sorry for me. I guess I want to show him I'm fine, so that when he leaves, this time it'll be for good and I can get used to it again.

I stash the extra weed my guy gave me into my *GTA: Vice City* case and stick it back on the shelf.

When Nate arrives, I lead him upstairs to my room, not realizing he hasn't been back in here for years until he starts looking around at everything with wide eyes.

"Woah, this is exactly how I remember it," he says.

"No, I used to have Winnie the Pooh sheets."

He snorts. "It hasn't been that long. I remember playing *GTA* and *Fifa* up here."

"Yeah well, Stacie made me move the PS2 downstairs, remember? So she could play some stupid NHL game."

"Getting bullied by your little sister, Flannigan?"

"Oh no, we don't do that frat boy last name thing here."

Nate flops down onto my bed and spreads his legs, making himself comfortable. "You'll have to get used to it if your sister's going to be playing hockey in college."

"She's thirteen. She's not going anywhere yet."

Nate gives me a knowing look and I shy away from it. I'm good at hiding, but he knows me from a more vulnerable, less guarded time. Who knows what he can see in me that other people can't?

"You're going to miss her, aren't you?"

"Course I am, *asshole*, she's my sister."

I kick his foot so he has to close his legs. "Wanna watch a movie or something?"

"Still got *Jackass?*"

I snort. "What are you? Twelve?"

He punches me in the arm. For a second, I imagine play-fighting with him. We're not kids anymore and I haven't touched him in years. Who knows how fucking weird it would be now that we're adults. I lean away.

"I've got a few movies on my laptop, I'll see what's on there."

While I login, I can feel him looking over my shoulder. My neck gets hot at the thought of him seeing everything I have on my computer. It's hidden, very fucking hidden, but still. Who knows what kind of computer courses he does up at that fancy school? I make a mental note not to leave him alone in my room for too long.

"Wanna just watch a comedy or something?" I let him see the movies on the screen, trying to ignore the fact I can hear him breathing. Smell some sort of spicy cologne on his clothes.

"Adam Sandler? And I'm twelve?"

"Well, you choose then." I shove the laptop toward him, but he just laughs.

"I'm kidding, that one looks good."

I put the movie on and rest the laptop on the desk by the bed.

"Can you see alright?"

"Yeah, you?"

"Yeah."

I know he can probably see me from the corner of his eye while he's watching the movie. Something about it puts me on edge.

I hope I've picked something that doesn't have any guys making out. We watched one once where two guys started going at it in an Adam Sandler movie and neither of us knew where to look. It was worse for me because I'd probably jerked off the night before thinking about Nate. I clear my throat.

"You want a drink? I'm gonna get something."

"Sure, if you're getting something, I'll have whatever."

I don't realize I haven't been letting myself breathe properly until I get half way down the stairs and suck in a full breath.

I don't want him here. It's too much like old times that don't fucking exist anymore. Those days are over. I'm not that kid anymore. There's the me before my dad got sick and the me after. There's no going back to the old one. Nate's just a reminder of everything I've lost.

I bring him a drink and some snacks and try to watch the rest of the movie and not think about anything. When I glance over to where the snacks are, I catch Nate watching me and I swear there's a bulge in his pants.

He shuffles when he sees me looking and he's so fucking obvious. It wasn't over me, I know that, but what the fuck was he getting a chub on for? Adam Sandler? Nate is not gay. I'd know. I remember that stupid crush he had on Amanda Harper at school. How much he'd blush and act like an idiot any time she walked by.

We watch the rest of the movie in awkward silence, neither one moving to grab a snack.

As soon as the credits roll, Nate stands up and says he has to leave for some fraternity thing. I don't know if he's bullshitting or not, but he's not hard anymore. I nod and don't bother walking him out as he leaves.

I CLEAR the food away and put everything back downstairs before logging onto the app on my phone. I need to get Nate and his unexplained hard-on out of my head.

I haven't been online to do this for a while. There was a time when I was addicted and would go on nearly every night, meeting different guys every time, going wherever they told me to meet them. Getting in the car with them and letting them take me wherever they wanted, without even asking where we were going. Sometimes it was deep into the woods, to let them fuck me against a tree or on the ground in the freezing cold—sometimes with a blanket or towel, sometimes not. Most of the time, we just stayed in their car and they fucked me on the backseat. One time we were close to being caught. That scared the shit out of me. I thought about what it would do to my dad to find out on his deathbed his only son had been caught getting fucked by some guy twice his age in the backseat of a Ford fucking Escort. But it didn't scare me enough to stop doing it. What's been stopping me these days is a lack of desire. Now a reminder of every horny teenage fantasy I had has been dropped into my life and I need to get it out.

A guy showing his bare chest with faded tattoos and the kind of muscles that probably used to be more impressive piques my interest. He's probably married, which is usually a good sign. Won't want to see you again. Wants to get it over with quickly. Though they're usually the most worried about mess.

I ask him to turn his camera on so I can see his face. My face isn't on here either, and he agrees so I'll turn my camera on, too.

He's not bad looking. Grey hair neatly trimmed with a matching beard. He doesn't look as old as his grey hair would suggest. I'd rather he leave it like that than dye it.

He tells me I'm very pretty.

Whatever. "Where can we meet?"

"I can pick you up near where you are."

"You know the woods by the boardwalk?" I start to describe the spot, but he knows it well already.

Another good sign. He knows what he's doing.

I try not to linger on the fact he's probably deceiving some poor woman at home as I get my keys and jacket and lock up. I don't want my ma to see me going out and asking questions.

I have to wait twenty minutes for him to show up and I'm freezing by the time his headlights dim as he pulls up the dark street.

The car's a big, fancy SUV. I hope this means we can do it inside.

I climb in the passenger side and he says hey and looks me over like I'm a piece of meat. I don't look at him. I don't care that much what he looks like anymore.

He keeps his eyes on the road as he drives. I've warmed up after a few minutes in the car with his heating on full blast.

"You said on your profile you like to bottom."

I grunt a response.

"That's good. It's unusual. You don't tend to get guys like you bottoming. I usually have to just take whatever's on offer."

I need him to stop talking. To distract myself and block his voice out, I glance at his hands on the steering wheel. His fingers are chubbier than his body. Wedding band digging in on the left hand, like it's been there a while and he hasn't tried to take it off in years.

There's a little part of me that wants to change my mind as the road starts to get darker and smaller, more isolated. Not because I think he's gonna hurt me. But because a little reminder of who I was before all this, before my dad got sick, has been dropped into my life. I have to remind myself that Nate isn't a part of my world anymore. Him being around is an interlude. This is my reality now.

"Shall we get in the backseat?"

I nod and free myself from the seatbelt, following him out of the car.

The wind whips my face as soon as I open the door and

I'm relieved again that I won't be lying on the floor of the woods with my bare ass out tonight.

Any lingering effect of seeing Nate today dies as soon as I get closer to what's gonna happen. *This* is what I need. *This* makes me forget. Not reliving old memories with childhood friends. *Fuck that.*

He gets a towel out of the trunk and drapes it over the backseat.

"Shall we just get straight to it?"

We kneel, facing each other as we unzip ourselves. I turn around as I pull my pants down and he awkwardly moves in behind me.

The contact of his bare thighs against mine sends a shiver down my spine and then his big clammy hands are on my hips, his breath loud and hot on the back of my neck. I don't know if I'm disgusted or turned on. A bit of both, I guess. As always.

I hear him pop a tube.

"Condom," I say.

"Of course," he grumbles with a laugh. "I'm not gonna bareback some kid I found online in the back of my car, that's just asking for trouble."

Kid?

"I'm twenty."

"Figure of speech. Ready?"

"Yeah."

His fingers are warm and slick as he slides them between my cheeks. I close my eyes and try to relax. Think about the moment when he makes me forget. When my head will be so consumed with his cock in my ass, I won't be able to think about anything else.

He presses against my back so I bend forward and slides his fingers deep inside me. I groan.

"That's it," he says, breathing heavy.

I don't give a fuck what he thinks of me. That's why I choose these guys. I'm never gonna see them again. If I do, they'll be with their wives and be more ashamed than I am. Or they'll be too shy to talk to me, knowing I'm too young for them. That it's never gonna happen again.

I hear him put the condom on but still twist around to check.

He lines his cock up with my hole and starts edging in. I'm turned on enough now to relax and he gets halfway in and I start stroking my cock so I don't lose my hard-on when he pushes all the way in the first time and I feel that initial sting.

He bottoms out and *fuck. There it is.* The memory eraser. No more feelings. Nothing. Just fireworks going off in my head. Steamed over windows. A stranger's breath on my neck and his hands gripping against my hips as he fucks me into the backseat. I don't listen to what he says. Some people are talkers, others are completely silent until they come. But I'm not thinking about him. I'm not thinking. That's the point.

Sometimes they think they want you to respond, but they don't. They're not thinking about you either. You're just a hole to fuck. A pound of flesh that feels good to stick their dick in. Nothing more. The second it's over, you'll be less than worthless to them.

He speeds up, grunts getting louder and less sporadic, his hands holding on tighter to my hips. I stroke myself faster, wanting to come before he finishes. They very rarely wanna touch you once they've finished. And blow jobs are awkward in the back of cars, even SUVs. I didn't come here for a shitty hand job I could have done better myself.

His beard brushes the back of my neck, his warm breath

on my skin as he mutters to himself. I pump my fist hard and fast around my dick until I feel myself coming. My muscles contracting around his cock. He starts spasming behind me, slapping my ass and calling out something I can't catch and couldn't give less of a shit about, because my world has gone still. I'm floating between reality and something else.

He snaps the condom off and zips up. When he opens his door, the night air rushes in and cools the sweat on my skin. I sit back and pull my pants back up, feeling the lube wet the seat of my boxers.

We sit in silence as he drives me back to where he picked me up. Putting the heaters back on to get the steam off the windows. Sweat drips down my arms from my pits and I watch his sweaty hands on the steering wheel as he drives. The wedding band glistening and the smell of sex in the air.

When he stops, he doesn't look at me. I stopped existing to him the second he blew his load inside that condom.

I'm about to climb out of the car, when he tells me to wait.

He digs into his pocket for something, finding a wallet and fishing out a few bills. My stomach churns. Is he really gonna pay me for sex? I open my mouth to tell him I'm not a fucking whore. But then I see the two fifties on the dashboard. Think about that cash I had to replace with my own money because the guys dipped into my supply. This would cover it and then some. My stomach drops and I'm grateful this asshole is looking anywhere but at me as I take it.

My ma's awake when I get home. I try to avoid her and go straight up to my room, but she catches me and asks me to come back downstairs.

I'm desperate to clean this lube out of my ass and this man's sweat off my skin. I don't want her to know what I did. What I've done over and over with so many men I've lost count. I don't want her to stop looking at me like I'm still that innocent kid who would have never imagined himself doing the things I do now. This guy wasn't the first to offer me money. But he's the first one to catch me desperate enough to accept.

"Where have you been out this late?" She has her hands on her hips at the counter. I'm not in the mood for one of her lectures. It's a little late for it now.

I open the fridge and look for the juice to distract myself and cool my face down.

"Evan, look at me while I'm talking to you."

"What?" I snap. I try to look away, but she grabs my face and turns it towards her.

"Talk to me. Why are you so angry?"

I can't look her in the eye. I don't want her to look at me. I don't want her to touch me. Tears sting the back of my eyes.

"Evan," she says, her voice soft as she pulls me in for a hug. I think she's gonna smell him on me. Smell the sex—lube and sweat and some married man's cum. I push her away and she bumps into the counter. We stare at each other for a second and I'm not sure who's more surprised.

"I'm sorry, Ma," I say finally. "Just, please, don't touch me."

"Okay." She holds her hands up, fixes her hair. "Okay, I'm sorry."

I slam the fridge door and run upstairs.

7

NATHAN

I toss and turn in bed, trying to get comfortable. The guys who room on my hall are all getting an early night for classes and practice or whatever in the morning, so it's pretty quiet around here. Too quiet.

The frat's mostly made up of guys from the tennis team and academic overachievers. The football team either dodges fraternities altogether or join a more party-oriented one. This fraternity is all about country clubs and "community service"—bullshit for "padding our resumés and advancing our careers." So we don't have many wild parties. I'm usually in bed by ten. Falling asleep as soon as my head hits the pillow. But tonight, I can't switch my thoughts off enough to relax.

My phone buzzes and I pull it out to see who the message is from. No one messages me at this time of night.

You up?

My heart pounds as my thumb works at the screen.

Yeah. What's up?

Where are you?

I'm …

I start to type out *at the frat house*, but stop. The fraternity seems to be the thing Evan's most mad about. The thing he finds most ridiculous about my new life.

I'm at home. Everything OK?

I fucked up.

Blood rushes in my ears. Panic at the possibility of Evan being in trouble. Then pleasure I know is selfish, because he chose to reach out to me of all people.

What happened?

There's no reply for what feels like an eternity. Then:

Doesn't matter

Go to sleep Nate

I'm up the second I read that last message. Turning the lamp on and squinting from the light while I try to find my socks and a pair of sweats to throw on.

I don't think it through. Just get dressed and leave the house on autopilot.

Adrenaline rushes through my veins as I drive as fast as the speed limit will allow all the way to my old neighborhood. I'd avoided it for years, but I've been back at least three times in the past few weeks.

It's only when I pull up outside Evan's house that I realize I don't have a plan.

I can't ring the doorbell and wake his mom and Stacie up. I can't get round the back of the house to throw a stone at his bedroom window without literally breaking in.

And if this neighborhood's still the way it was when I was a kid, the cops will be called the second I breach the fence.

I stay in the driver's seat with the headlights off and try messaging him instead.

Evan

I'm outside.

What the fuck?

I tiptoe across the hall, trying not to wake my ma or Stacie. Pull the blinds to the side and spot Nate's big black SUV parked at the end of the driveway.

My phone buzzes again.

If you don't come out I'm ringing the doorbell

I panic, but I know he won't do that. He's way too much of a brown nose to risk pissing my ma off. Why the fuck did I text him of all people? I had a moment of weakness and he was the first person who came to mind. The only one I could tell that I'd fucked up who might actually care.

I throw my sneakers on and a hoodie and go outside, the cold air biting at my bare legs in my shorts as I make my way down the driveway to Nate's car.

He gets out, his hair messy under a fucking backward baseball cap. A Princeton t-shirt and grey sweats. My mouth gets dry, nervous from how good he looks, and I have to remind myself he's a fucking frat boy. An Ivy League asshole. I don't fuck with guys like that.

"Hey," he whispers when I get close enough to hear him.

I try to be angry. To spit the words, but when I speak, I sound like a little kid.

"What the fuck are you doing here, Nate?"

He shrugs. "You sounded like you needed to talk."

"It's the middle of the night."

"So?"

There's this big fucking part of me that just wants to go with him, wherever he's going. Ask him to take me to his nice house, where all his clothes are clean and his Nikes are brand new. Let me live in his crisp, tennis-white world. But the other part of me, the smart bit, knows that's not possible.

"You've done what Ma asked you to do." I spit. "You can go home now."

He shakes his head. "I'm not doing that, Evan. *You* texted me."

Hearing him say my name, *fuck.*

"Forget it. I didn't want you to come over here."

He ignores me. "Is Frankie's still open?"

That word instantly brings me back, like no time has passed at all. And for a second, everything shucks off my shoulders and I snort. "You're kidding right? That place'll survive the apocalypse."

He smiles. "Get in."

He starts climbing into the car before I even have a chance to reply. I could ignore him. Turn around and walk back into the house. I consider it for a second. Consider going back to bed, alone, with nothing but my thoughts and memories of that guy's breath on my neck. The sting of him inside me. The greasy fifty-dollar bills burning a hole in that shoebox under my bed.

Nate switches the engine on and the dashboard lights up his face. He glances over, meeting my gaze, and for a second, the frat boy in the driver's seat of his Beemer is my Nate again.

The car has a pine tree scent, but as Nate backs out of the driveway, I catch something else. It's him. His sweat and the way he'd smell when he slept in my bed all night and woke up with his hair stuck to his face. He was in bed when I texted, and he got up, came all the way out here, for me.

My gut churns and my pulse speeds up while I try not to look at the shape of his thighs in those grey sweats. Remind myself that this doesn't mean shit. It doesn't make up for all those years. For what he did, or let someone else do, back then. If I ever needed proof he didn't give enough of a shit about me, about our friendship, then he gave it to me that night.

The stereo is on low, playing some rock song. It's too quiet for me to recognize what it is.

"Want me to put something on?" he asks, gesturing to the speaker.

"Nah, I'm good."

It's weird watching Nate drive a car. The way he handles the SUV with ease. I don't even have a license, though my dad taught me to drive. It's kind of ironic that Nate is the responsible car owner now.

His light brown hair pokes out from under the backward cap, and I can see the Princeton 'P' from this angle. I try to focus on it, remind myself that Nate's in a totally different world now. *He doesn't know you, couldn't understand you anymore.*

. . .

Frankie's is coming up on the corner. The F in the neon sign used to flicker, now it's completely broken and the sign says '*rankie's*'. The place looks like a shit hole, but the food's good and I've never heard of anyone getting sick off it.

Nate parks the car and I don't even wanna joke about it getting jacked here. I guess his stepdad'll pay for it if it does. He doesn't look worried.

We go in, the bell dinging above the door. It's a familiar scene: a tired waitress in an old-fashioned diner uniform glances up from filing her nails at the counter. A couple of old men nurse cups of coffee. A trucker reads the newspaper in a booth with a plate of scrambled eggs in front of him.

We take a booth a couple of rows away from the trucker and start looking at the menu. It feels weird sitting here with Nate. For a second, I imagine telling him everything. Why I let those men fuck me. How it makes me feel. How I hate myself after and how I wish I could stop. How sometimes I hope for something else I know I can't have or that doesn't exist.

But then he smiles at me over his menu and I don't wanna see the look of disgust on his face when he finally knows me.

"Chili cheese fries?"

I hesitate. I don't have any cash.

"My treat," he says, trying to smile.

"You don't need to buy me food," I growl.

He rolls his eyes. "I dragged you out of the house in your shorts. It's not charity. Relax."

I take a deep breath, imagine refusing and sitting here in silence without even a plate of fries to distract me. "Fine ... thanks."

He's quiet while we wait for our food. I try not to stare at his hands on the table. Try to block out the sound of his car keys jingling when he shifts on his seat.

When the waitress puts our food down in front of us, Nate immediately starts pigging out—exactly like when we were kids and we'd save up enough money to split a milkshake and a side of fries. Nate was always a pushover. Always let me eat the last fry or slurp up the last of the milkshake.

Now, he sits back in the booth, groaning and rubbing his belly.

"I never eat stuff like this anymore. Coach Sanchez has us on a strict diet."

"I still can't believe you play fucking tennis," I say, reaching for a fry.

The tips of his ears get pink.

"Me, neither."

Smearing chili sauce around the plate, I keep my eyes down as I ask, "Do you like it?"

"Sure."

I look up fast enough to catch the shrug.

"'Sure?' Sounds like a lot of hard work for something you're not that into."

"I like it," he admits.

I nod, stuffing the fry in my mouth. "You got friends up there at that fancy school?"

He scoffs. "Yeah, a few."

"So why are you sitting here eating greasy diner food on the bad side of town with me?"

Something flutters in my stomach while I wait for his answer. What the fuck do I think he's gonna say?

I'd rather be here with you? You're better than them?

Yeah, right.

He shrugs again. "You needed me, so I came."

Somehow that's both better and worse than what I was imagining he'd say.

I bite back the response that sits on the tip of my tongue —*I've needed you for the past five years, where were you then?*

I push the fries into the middle of the table and sit back.

"Evan ... " Nate takes a deep breath and wipes his hands on a napkin. "If you want to talk, about your dad-"

"I don't."

"Okay." He nods. "But if you ever do...."

"Listen Nate, I don't need your fucking counselling, okay?"

He looks up at me with those big green eyes.

"*Fuck,* why do you have to give me that Bambi shit?"

"What?" His lips twitch up on one side and I have to grit my teeth to stop from mirroring the smile.

"I'm not giving you the 'Bambi shit.'" He shakes his head. "I'm just trying to be a friend."

"Because my ma asked you to babysit me."

"No, not because of that." He looks down at the table, running his finger through some salt grains. "Evan, I know I haven't been here...."

I start to sweat. My heart racing. How long have I waited for Nate to come back and tell me how sorry he was for leaving? How much he's missed me? How wrong I was about him thinking he's better than me now? But I can't take it. Whatever he has to say, I don't wanna hear it. Not anymore. It's too late.

I cut him off before he can even try.

"You screwed me over back then, but I'm over it," I say, shoving another fry in my mouth. "Believe it or not, the world doesn't revolve around you, and I haven't just been sitting in my room moping. I've had bigger things to think about."

"More coffee, hon?"

Nate had been staring at me with those big stupid Bambi eyes, but he flinches at the waitress' voice. He looks too stunned to speak, so I answer for him. "No, thanks."

She shrugs and walks away.

"Shouldn't you get back to the frat house? Won't your brothers be wondering where you've gone?"

He opens his mouth to say something but closes it again before nodding. My heart sinks. Once again, he let it go, just like that. No fighting. I shouldn't be surprised. I can't compete with the lifestyle he has now. I don't even blame him for choosing it over me anymore. I want him to have it. He deserves it. Always has. The other side of all this shit is where he was always supposed to be.

Nate waits until he's started the car and is pulling out of Frankie's to ask what he probably came over to ask in the first place.

"You said something happened? In your message, you said you fucked up."

I swallow, think about telling him to mind his own business, but it feels redundant seeing as I started this.

"I pissed my ma off, it's not a big deal. I overreacted."

Nate nods. Swallows. His Adam's apple bobbing in his smooth throat.

"What did you two argue over?"

"Nothing, she was hassling me, I shouldn't have lost it with her. I pushed her, I didn't hurt her but ... I should have done it."

"Evan, you're grieving, you-"

"It's fine, alright?"

He takes in a sharp breath and nods. "Okay, if you say so."

8

NATHAN

After I take Evan back to our old neighborhood, I drive for a while in the opposite direction from the frat house. I should go home and get some sleep, but I'll just lie there staring at the ceiling and people will be getting up soon. Putting the blender on to make smoothies. Arguing over who gets the best shower. I just can't face it right now.

What did he mean I 'screwed him over?' I know I messed up back then. My stupidity got us both into trouble and Evan got most of the blame, like always. But how was that my fault? He told me not to say anything. I was just doing what he told me to do. I wanted to remind him of that, but it felt wrong. With everything that's happened to him since I left, it didn't feel right to argue.

Sitting with Evan in Frankie's up to that point ... it felt like old times. Except there was this ghost between us. And worst of all, Evan was like a ghost too. Something's missing in him. That mischief and *life* he had when we were growing up. My stomach drops when I consider the possibility that it's gone forever.

I pull the SUV into an empty parking lot and take a nap until a security guard taps on the window and tells me I can't sleep here.

When I check the time on my dashboard, it's almost 9am. *Shit.*

I drive as fast as I can back to the house to get my tennis bag. No one's home when I get there—everyone's already at classes or practice. I haven't even had time to change my clothes or take a shower.

When I get to the tennis center, everyone's already out on the courts, warming up. I rush into the locker room and change into my tennis clothes. Only looking up from lacing my shoes to find Coach Sanchez standing in the doorway with his arms crossed over his chest.

"You're late, Nathan."

"I know, I'm sorry Coach. It won't happen again."

He's still watching me carefully after I've laced my shoes up and grabbed my racket out of my bag.

"Is something going on?"

My neck flushes. "Like what?"

"I don't know." He shrugs. "You've never been late to practice before. And you look like hell. Is there something I should be worried about? Is there something you need to talk to someone about?"

"No, Coach."

He looks me over again. "You look like you've been out all night. Were you drinking?"

"Of course not. I just slept through my alarm."

He nods, but I can see he doesn't believe me.

"You know you can come to me with any problems, right?"

"Yes Coach. Thank you. Like I said, it won't happen again."

When I get out onto the court, Priestley's giving me the stink eye and Ben's trying to throw me a sympathetic smile.

Fuck, how did I let this happen?

Even now I'm here, I can't focus. Everyone's already paired up so Assistant Coach Rodriguez hits with me, but I miss everything and can't even get my serve locked in. He jogs up to the net and asks me if I'm okay, basically repeating Coach Sanchez's little speech. I tell him I'm fine. I can't wait until we can get off the court and I can be left alone.

I'm never like this. I love tennis. Even practice. Love being out here on the crisp blue courts with the sun beating down on my back. The rhythmic sound of tennis balls hitting rackets. Laughter from my teammates. The camaraderie. The team spirit. But I don't feel it today.

Priestley approaches me the second we get into the locker room, repeating my coaches' questions, but with less concern.

"You know this game against Harvard is important, right?"

"I know that."

"Give him a break, Priestley. He was probably just out getting laid," Archer chimes in, pulling a t-shirt over his head.

Priestley sighs and rolls his eyes. "No one asked you."

"Hey, when we're in the locker room, only Coach can tell me what to do."

"That sounds dirty." Miles grins.

"Ew, shut up."

My face flushes, but Priestley at least lets me go.

I TEXT EVAN.

What are you doing later?

No reply comes and I tell myself he's probably asleep. Not ignoring me.

I can't let this go. I need to talk to him. We need to get all of this out in the open. Talk about what happened. Make him let me explain. Apologize. And if he still doesn't listen, if he still wants to resent me, then fine. There's nothing else I can do after that.

I make it through the day. My business class with Ben—who is good enough not to question me on why I was late to practice. A meeting at the frat house I sit through on autopilot, until Priestley calls on me to provide some documents I luckily worked on already last week.

I keep checking my phone whenever I can. But there's no reply from Evan. Unable to wait around anymore, the second the meeting is over, I hop in my car and head over to my old neighborhood, sending a message to Evan on the way.

I'm coming over, meet me at the beach? Our old spot where the good shells used to be. I know you're mad, but please, I just want one chance to explain.

While I drive, I can almost smell the sand and hear the clack of shells in buckets we were bringing home for our moms. Evan's salty skin as we stood under the outdoor showers and washed sand off our feet. While I averted my eyes and tried not to get excited over Evan being so close and so almost-naked.

I look at my phone at every stop sign and light, but there's no reply from Evan.

After getting no response, I don't expect to find him at

our spot. But when I stop the car, there he is, sitting on a boulder with a hoodie on and his back to the road.

The minute I see him, I know I'm fucked. I would have run through fire to be here right now, and not just because he needs me. Or someone. But because ever since I saw him again at his dad's funeral, even though it was the shittiest of circumstances, I haven't been able to stop thinking about him.

He's staring out at the black water.

"What's up?" I ask, taking a seat beside him on the sand.

He looks over at me and snorts.

I frown. "What?"

"You're wearing a fucking tie."

My face flushes. "I had a meeting at the fraternity. Everyone wears suits for them." I loosen the tie self-consciously and shuffle my weight on the boulder. "How's everything with you?"

He's quiet for so long, I don't think he's going to answer. Finally he clears his throat.

"You said you wanted to explain. So here I am. Explain. And then leave me and my family the fuck alone. The last thing Stace and Ma need is you coming back and hurting them. They've already lost enough."

"I ... " *Fuck.* "I'm sorry, Evan."

He looks disappointed. And I know at this point, sorry isn't enough.

"I'm sorry, but we were just kids. You know I didn't mean to get you into trouble. I didn't mean any of it, it was just a stupid mistake."

"It's not the mistake though, Nate. I know you didn't mean to fuck up but you stole a fucking car."

"I know that, and I wish I could take it back, I-"

"That's not what I'm pissed about, and if you can't even see what you did wrong...."

Frustration bubbles until I'm standing, looking down at him and speaking in a voice that's way more high-pitched than my normal voice. "So tell me then. Stop making me guess, just fucking tell me."

He squints, like he's trying to figure out if I'm for real. "You really don't know?"

"Know what?"

"Nate, you threw me under the fucking bus. Your stepdad's fancy lawyer nearly got me thrown in juvie. They made me look like a fucking delinquent. They said it was all my idea. That I 'influenced' you to do it."

My heart drops. My blood going cold.

"What?"

"I never expected your stepdad to pay for my lawyer, but I didn't expect you to sell me out like that. You could have got off on the charges without feeding me to the fucking sharks."

"Evan, I ... " I scramble back down to the seat next to him, reaching for him before thinking better of it. He flinches from my touch. "I didn't know, I swear, you've got to believe me, I would have never ... " It's like a switch has been flipped in my head. Relief and dread rushing through me at once. So that's why he ghosted me? I really did screw him over, and I didn't even know.

Evan's face has softened, but he still won't look at me. When he speaks, it's practically a mumble. "It doesn't matter now anyway."

"It does. I can make it better."

He scoffs. "How you gonna do that, Nate? You got a time machine in the trunk of that fancy-ass car?"

My face floods with heat. "Okay, I deserve that. But you've got to know I didn't choose this, any of it."

He sighs, shaking his head. "I'm not blaming you for accepting his money. I'd do the same in your place. Someone tried to give me a Beemer? An Ivy League education? Yeah, I'd take that shit too." He looks down, his face flushing. "But I'd never sell my friend out for it."

"Neither would I!"

He shakes his head, turning his body away from me before wiping sand off his legs and standing up. "I don't know what you want from me, Nate."

"I don't want anything. I just want to be there for you."

"You don't have to be. It's done. Forget it. You told me you didn't know, and I believe you. You can go back to your frat bros and your fancy college with a clear conscience."

I try to reach for him, but he flinches from my touch again, like I burned him.

"Just leave me alone, yeah."

His tone cuts right through me. Have I really hurt him that much?

9

EVAN

I need to get Nate out of my head—whatever the fuck that was last night. It doesn't matter if he knew or not. He had to know *something* like that had happened. Either that or he chose to stick his head in the sand, because I know he's not stupid. It might be easier if he was. Even if he didn't know about what his stepdad did to me, he still blanked me on the boardwalk that day with his friends. How can he explain that away?

He'll stop trying after a while. That's if he hasn't stopped already. Just like last time. It took three unreturned messages and he was gone. It was too easy for him to be tempted by his stepdad's money and the promise of being a part of some elite club. What the fuck do I have to offer him that his new world can't give him ten times over?

I work my shift at the warehouse, dodging Bob so he doesn't ask me about that stupid course again. Leave.

When I get home, Ma's already in bed and behind her bedroom door, I can hear Stacie on the phone with her friend. I think about going in and telling her to go to sleep, but I don't like the idea of taking on that role. She doesn't need me trying to be her dad.

There's an empty hanger on the back of Ma's bedroom door and it forces me to stop dead. An empty hanger shouldn't mean shit. For years, Dad's work clothes would be on the back of that hanger, waiting for him to get up in the morning and put them on. Even after he stopped being able to go to work regularly, he or my mom left the hanger there—maybe some kind of hope that eventually things would go back to normal. Except they didn't. He hadn't been able to work for years before he died, so why the fuck am I thinking about that now? Something twists in my chest and I push it down, opening the door to my own room.

I login to the app I use to meet guys. There are always people online, looking for a hookup, whether it's 1am or 1pm. It's sad. The desperation of the married men, up at 1am while their wives are asleep. The loneliness of the single men, desperate for a little human interaction.

Nate's face comes back to me, staring at me with those big eyes. How immature he is. He wouldn't know the first thing about being desperate, being lonely. He doesn't even fucking know how to live in the adult world yet. He's still wrapped up in his little bubble of college life. Clubs, teams, fraternities, whatever the fuck he belongs to. Nate was always supposed to belong. Well, he does now. He's where he's supposed to be.

I tell myself this, but every man who pops up turns me off. I don't want them. But I don't want Nate, either. Why did he have to fucking come back? I'd put him out of my head. Told myself he didn't even exist anymore. But he does. There are glimmers of the old Nate in there. All grown up. Parts of him I don't know yet, but want to.

I'm fucked.

I lie back on my bed and put my headphones on, trying to get him out of my head. But I can still see Nate's face in profile. That little bump in his nose from when he broke it trying to jump a car on a homemade ramp. The scar on his top lip you'd only see if you knew to look, from when he snagged it on barbed wire, climbing a fence to get to a box of popsicles they were throwing out of Walmart. And that little scar in his eyebrow, from when he crashed that fucking car and called me to come help him.

His stupid-ass backward cap with the Ivy League logo. The clean polo shirt and neatly trimmed nails, freshly shaven face. It barely hid the Nate I knew last night. I could see him. Sitting next to me on the beach in the dark. All I could see were the scars I remember *my* Nate getting. The way he smiled. That unique smell I used to feel ashamed of sniffing in the t-shirts he'd sleep in and leave behind at my house.

I can see myself reaching across the gearstick and running my hand up the inside of his thigh. Watching a blush spread across his cheeks as his sweats get tight around his swelling dick.

I think about his lips as I slide my hand into my boxers. My cock is rock hard before I've even touched it. Imagining Nate's breath on my face. The shocked look I bet he gets on his face just before he comes. I bite my lip, so I'm not tempted to say his name as I spill over my hand.

THERE ARE voices floating up from downstairs. The sun floods around the blinds and my t-shirt's stuck to me with sweat, and, *fuck*, dried cum.

I slip into the bathroom just as laughter erupts up the

stairs. My whole body floods with warmth, my guts churning at the sound of Nate's voice.

What the fuck is he doing here? In my *house? Laughing with my ma and sister?*

I have to stop myself from going down there, but if anyone'll recognize the smell of dried cum, it's a frat boy.

I turn the dial on the shower as cold as I can take it. My skin gets red and blotchy under the icy spray and I wash as fast as I can.

When I get downstairs, dressed in a clean t-shirt and sweats, Nate's still sitting at the kitchen table, a plate of my ma's half-eaten pancakes in front of him.

"Morning, baby," Ma says when she sees me. "Want some pancakes?"

I grunt a response before taking the only seat between Stacie and Nate.

"Hey," Nate says. He squares his shoulders, like he's expecting a fight, before tucking back into his breakfast. "I just came to say hi to your mom and Stacie." He looks up again, meeting my eye, his gaze is penetrating now. I know what he's doing. He wants to show me that I'm wrong about him. That no matter what happened between us, he's not gonna let them down—not this time.

"Don't you have tennis practice or frat meetings to be at?"

"Evan!" Ma scolds me from the stove.

Nate smiles, but the confident act is slipping a little. He's stopped eating and he's just pushing the pancakes around now. "No. Just a class this afternoon."

"What did you say you were studying, Nate?" Ma asks. She brings a plate of pancakes over and puts them down in front of me.

"Business and economics."

"Oh wow. Are you gonna start your own business when you graduate?"

He squirms a little. "I'd like to. Me and a friend of mine —Ben—have this idea about starting something where tennis players connect with coaches and nutritionists and trainers and things like that. We want to open more tennis courts in low-income areas and get sponsors for kids from all backgrounds to help them get into tennis."

Hearing him say 'low-income areas' makes my blood boil. But I won't make a scene in front of Ma and Stacie. I shovel a bite of food in my mouth.

"That's amazing, Nate," Ma says.

"Yeah, really cool," Stacie agrees.

"How about your stepdad, what does he do again?" Ma takes a sip of coffee. She's looking at Nate like he's the most interesting thing in the world. I wanna tell her he's not that special, but I can't even fucking say it in my head.

"His company buys other companies and then tells them how to make more money. I don't really know, to be honest." Nate's voice is tense. I remember him hating his stepdad when his ma first met him. But I'm guessing he's over it now. The guy gave him this awesome life, with all his awesome frat bros, and awesome tennis clubs, and all the awesome money he could ever want.

"Could he help out with some of this stuff? Getting your idea off the ground?"

Nate turns bright red. *Knew it. Stepdaddy comes to the rescue once again.*

"Um, yeah. He's put me in touch with some people who could point us in the right direction."

Point you in the right direction? Like fund it and push it to the front of the line. Nepotism at its finest.

"I keep telling Evan he should start a business," Ma says.

I nearly spit my pancakes all over the table. If only she knew the kind of business I was in on the side.

Stacie scoffs.

"What?" Ma asks.

"Evan's a dumbass."

I know she's a kid and that's what siblings do, but *fuck you little girl.*

"He is not a dumbass," Ma says.

"True," Nate says.

What the fuck?

He leans over the table, close enough that I can smell his expensive cologne and the maple-flavor syrup on his breath. "Evan is actually a secret nerd. At school, he'd always get the highest score in the pop quizzes Mrs. Smith set us. They were really hard, too."

Ma's fucking beaming. Stacie giggles and my face feels like it's on fire.

"Can everyone stop talking about me like I'm not here now?"

"What? It's true," Nate says, sinking back in his chair.

My heart races. Blood rushes in my ears. I push my chair back, the legs scraping loudly on the cheap vinyl floor.

"Where are you going?" Ma asks.

"Out."

I throw a hoodie on at the door, slip into my battered Nikes and leave the house, relief and guilt rushing through me as I move away from that place.

"Evan!"

I ignore Nate's voice and keep walking. He gets in his car and turns the engine. He'll catch up with me, easy. But the further away from the house I am, the better.

He drives alongside me as I round the corner out of the neighborhood.

"Get in," he says. "We'll go to the arcade."

I ignore him, keep walking.

"Or the movies. Or Frankie's. Or the beach."

I stop and the car moves past me before it comes screeching to a halt. He gets out, slamming the door behind him before blocking my way.

"Just stop, Nate."

"Stop what?"

"You know what. You did what Ma asked. I'm fine. You're free."

He keeps looking at me with those fucking Bambi eyes.

"I told you I'm not just here because your mom asked."

I turn back around, continuing down the sidewalk.

"Evan, wait!"

My heart thuds so hard against my chest it hurts.

I have to fix my face before I turn to face him. "What?"

"I miss you, okay?" He shrugs. "And listen, I know I'm lucky. And maybe I should have asked more questions back then, checked in more. I wish every day I hadn't just given up on you. And I know you think I fit in at Princeton, but the truth is, I'm half there and half here. And if I don't fit in here, then ... *fuck*. I don't know." He scrubs a hand over his face.

I just stare at him, in his brand new shoes and fucking designer polo. Trying to figure out what to say. Eventually I go with, "Fuck you, Nate."

His eyebrows shoot up. "What?"

"You don't get to just come back here and complain about your perfect fucking life."

Nathan

I watch him turn and walk away from me again and I know, somehow, that if I let him walk away, this time it'll be it.

"Shit." I follow him until I'm close enough to grab his arm.

"You wanna know the real reason I stayed away all these years? Why I let you ghost me like that without a fight?"

He spins around, nostrils flaring. "I fucking know why, Nate, you don't have to say it. I saw you that day on the boardwalk with your fancy friends and I know you saw me. You're embarrassed to be seen with me. Well, fine, I don't give a shit. Just go."

"What are you talking about? What day on the boardwalk?"

"Don't fucking lie. You saw me."

"I didn't, I swear!"

He shakes his head and walks away.

Fuck, fuck, fuck. I can't let him walk away again. Not now. Not like this. I hadn't realized how much I'd missed him until now. How lonely it's been to always be pretending. Fixing the way I speak. Putting on an act.

"Evan, I didn't see you. But you're right, I was embarrassed."

That stops him dead. His face has dropped when he turns around and I scramble to explain.

"I wasn't embarrassed by you, I was embarrassed by ... how I felt. About you. Why do you think I took that car? I wanted to impress you. I wanted to show you I could be a badass, like you. Like the guys in those games we played."

He's staring at me like he wants me to shut the fuck up. But I've started now, and at least if he never wants to speak to me again, I'll know it's for the right reason. At least I will have had a chance to give him the truth.

"I don't know if I'm bi or whatever. I've never thought about a guy like that, except ... you. And I don't ... I'm not here to ... I'm not asking anything from you, I don't expect anything. I just want to be your friend again. I miss that. Miss who I was back then, with you. You got me, the me before the money. The kid with the holes in his shoes." I try a smile, but Evan only looks angrier the more I talk. "So ... yeah." I slap my hands down by my sides. "Now you know. I abandoned you, but you abandoned me too. When you stopped returning my texts, I was a coward and I took the easy way out, because how I felt about you scared the shit out of me, and I knew I'd fucked up and I thought maybe you hated me. Or maybe you even knew I liked you and you were disgusted or something." I scan his face for clues as to whether I was right. By the utter shock and confusion etched into his features right now, I'm guessing I was wrong.

"And then I got a girlfriend, and for a while, I stopped thinking about guys. It was the coward's option, and I'm sorry I wasn't there for you when your dad was sick. I wish I had been. But I can't change that now. And Evan, we were kids. If I'd have known Bryce screwed you over, I would have done something about it, I swear. I would never throw you under the bus, not for anything."

I stop talking. Evan hasn't said a word. I swear he hasn't blinked since I started talking.

"Evan? Say something."

He swallows. Opens his mouth. Closes it again.

"I've gotta go."

"What?"

My heart sinks into my stomach as I watch him turn around, telling myself surely he can't just walk away after everything I just said. I want to call him back, but what would be the point? I told him. I put it all out there and he's made it clear what he thinks.

I get back in the car and start the engine, throwing one last glance in Evan's direction to see if maybe he changed his mind. But no. Even the sound of the engine purring to life doesn't make him turn around or alter his course. He's even further away now than he was before.

I'M NOT in any kind of mood to face people when I drive back to campus.

Ben's waiting for me outside class. I try to paint on my usual fake smile as I get out of the car with my books, but he sees straight through it.

"Hey, what's wrong?"

"Nothing. Let's go in, we're gonna be late."

I can feel him watching me while I try to listen to the professor and make notes. But I'm mostly just scribbling nonsense on the page and tuning out her voice.

After class, he won't take no for an answer until I agree to go for coffee with him. He waits until we're set up on some too-soft couches at the campus coffee shop to ask me what's wrong.

"Is it Mira?"

The thought is so far from my mind that it takes me a second to even register why I'd be upset over Mira.

"No, it's not Mira."

I can see he isn't going to let me off the hook until I tell him something. Looking around to see if anyone's listening, I lean in closer and he mirrors my posture.

"I've been hanging out with that friend, from my old neighborhood."

"Uh huh?" Ben's giving me his whole attention.

"And well ... he's mad at me for something I didn't even know Bryce did, when we were younger."

He frowns. "Why would he be mad at you if you didn't know? What did Bryce do?"

I sigh and lean in even closer, still ashamed of that stupid mistake and worried someone will overhear. "I stole a car and crashed it into a tree, and then, panicking, and not knowing what else to do, I called Evan. He came and cleaned up my mess."

Ben's eyes grow comically wide.

"Bryce hadn't been dating my mom for long at this point and she was furious. But he fixed it. He got some fancy lawyer and I got off without even a smudge on my record. I tried to talk to Evan about it after, find out what happened to him. But he ghosted me and I guess I was scared to find out, or scared he was mad at me or ..." I run a hand over my face. "Scared he'd realized how I felt about him."

Ben flushes. "What do you mean?" His voice is small.

I swallow. "I had a crush on him." There, it's out there. Out in the world to someone other than Evan. I can only hope Ben reacts better than Evan did.

He blinks hard a few times. I can see the effort it's taking him to maintain eye-contact. His blush making his cheeks blotchy.

"And I told him, this morning."

"Oh."

I sink back in my chair, the velvet upholstery almost swallowing me whole.

Ben frowns, looking down at his hands. For a second, I think my friend is going to reject me for coming out. My heart thuds. Not Ben. He's the last person who'd reject me for something like that. Surely?

Finally, he clears his throat. Re-arranging the expression on his face to something more neutral. "So what did he say?"

"Nothing." I sigh, relieved at least that he's not still sitting there in silence. I think about Evan's back as he walked away. My heart sinking all over again.

"He didn't say anything at all?"

I shake my head. "He just walked away. He said he had to go."

Ben sighs. "I'm sorry. That sucks."

I shrug.

"So are you like, gay, or...."

"I think I'm bi." My mouth's dry, but it feels good to say it. Telling Evan, it was the first time I said it out loud, and it sucks that's the reaction I got.

"That's cool." Ben nods.

I let out a nervous laugh.

"What?" he asks.

"Nothing. It's just, for a second there, I thought you were going to be mad."

He closes his eyes in a slow blink before answering. "Nate, I'm your friend. Why would I be mad?"

I shake my head. "I don't know, it's stupid I guess, it's just ... after Evan's reaction."

Ben leans closer, his eyes full of concern now. "What are you going to do?"

I shrug. "Nothing, what can I do? He made it pretty clear what he thinks about it. I'm not gonna stalk the guy."

He sinks back in his chair. "I'm sorry, Nate."

"It's not a big deal," I lie.

"Hey." His eyes brighten, his face turning beet red. "If you ever want me to be your wingman, at like a gay bar or whatever, I will be."

I laugh. "Thanks, but I don't think we'd get into a bar with your babyface."

His shoulders slump. "I do not have a babyface."

"Yeah, you kind of do. Anyway, I've never been into a guy other than Evan."

Ben frowns and stares at me, puzzled. "What do you mean?"

"I'm not sure." I squirm. It was easier to explain it to myself before I ever had to say it out loud. But Evan is the only guy I've ever thought about in that way. The only guy I've ever been attracted to.

"Have you ever tried to ... " Ben blushes. "You know, watch ... " he drops his voice so low I have to lean in to hear him. "Gay porn?"

For some reason, *I* blush. We're fraternity brothers who used to share a room. It's pretty stupid to get embarrassed talking about porn with the guy. But out of all my brothers, Ben is the most reserved when it comes to that stuff. I never walked in on him jerking off or watching porn, and he always stays quiet when the other guys talk about sex.

I shake my head.

"Maybe you should." He shrugs. "Maybe it'd help you figure some stuff out."

Ben lingers when we get back to the house, like he's babysitting me, making sure I'm okay. I appreciate it, but right now, I just want to be alone.

I make an excuse about being tired and go up to my room. At least I don't have to share anymore like I did when we first moved into the frat house. Ben's my best friend here, but he snores—and sometimes talks—in his sleep. Being woken up in the middle of the night by someone asking where their liver is gets old pretty quickly.

I open my laptop and make a big pretense of scrolling through my socials before clicking on what I really want to look at. I don't know why I try to fool myself that I didn't open my computer to look at porn.

I scroll through the usual videos of men and women, two women together. I don't want to type it into the search bar, but I realize after not accidentally landing on gay porn that I'll have to.

I type in 'bisexual curious' and a bunch of videos of women come up. I refine my search to 'bisexual curious men' and feel my heartrate quicken as the screen is filled with stills of naked men, doing stuff to each other.

I make sure my screen isn't facing the door and my volume is on low, so if someone does just walk into my room—which happens—at least they won't see *what* I'm looking at. I know I shouldn't be embarrassed, and I don't think I am. A little scared, sure. But I'm not that kid anymore who ran away from his best friend because he was scared of how he made him feel. I just want this to be private for now. Until I figure it out a little more.

I hover over a thumbnail of a guy with a shaved head, but before I can click on it, memories of Evan's face after I told him I had a crush on him come flooding back. I scroll past that clip. Landing on two generic guys with dark hair and similar faces.

The two of them sit on a couch in a sparsely decorated studio, pretending to play a video game. One of them is wearing a generic sport's jersey and the other a white tank top. Jersey says something about feeling kind of horny in the most wooden acting voice I've ever heard. Seconds later, they're all over each other, making out and grabbing each other's cocks through their sweatpants.

It's stupid and the acting is terrible. The set looks like it's going to fall down around their heads. But I'm so turned on, my cock is aching.

I unzip my chinos and slide my hand into my boxer briefs, stroking myself while I watch the two guys start to go down on each other.

I open the drawer beside my bed without taking my eyes off the screen and squeeze some lube out onto my hand before sliding it back in my pants. My cock looks obscene when I pull it out. Swollen and red and leaking already. I watch myself, the guys in the background, sliding my hand up and down the shaft, wondering what cock tastes like while the actors suck each other on the screen.

The camera zooms in on Tank Top's face, his lips stretched around Jersey's huge dick. Tank Top's eyes roll back like he's enjoying it and he moans around Jersey's erection. I bite my lip and hold in a groan as my hips buck off the bed.

Tank Top pulls off and starts licking the other guy's swollen head, lapping at the pre-cum beading from the other guy's slit.

"Mm," he says, pulling away. "That tastes so good."

"I knew you wanted my cock," Jersey says.

Holy fuck, this is hot.

Tank Top gets back to work, taking Jersey all the way into his throat, his eyes watering as he gags. Jersey growls and fists Tank Top's hair as he thrusts into his mouth. Jersey pulls out, rubbing the head of his cock across Tank Top's swollen lips and I want to shout at the screen for him to put his dick back in his mouth already. I was so close.

But then Jersey bends Tank Top over the table and a

bead of pre-cum leaks out of my slit. I rub my thumb over it and shiver.

Tank Top has this blissed-out look on his face while Jersey spits in his crack and starts fingering his ass. Jersey pulls his cheeks apart and the camera gives us a close-up I think was filmed at another time, the angle's all wrong, but it doesn't matter.

I didn't think I was into close-ups of other men's assholes, but....

The camera zooms in on Jersey's face between the other guy's cheeks. He's moving his face, his nose brushing against the top of the guy's crack, and it stupidly takes me a second to realize what he's doing.

Oh ... ohhh.

Tank Top, still bent over the table, is letting out the filthiest, most blissed-out moans I've ever heard. With one more stroke, I come all over my hand and chest.

Fuck. They didn't even start fucking each other yet and I came at the sight of someone eating out someone's ass.

I slam the laptop shut and go to clean up.

WE'RE HOSTING Harvard tennis the next day, so at least there's enough distraction to keep my mind off Evan for a while.

I get to the locker room early to have a moment to compose myself before the guys arrive. Try to soak up where I am. Remind myself of what Bryce said. I'm getting the opportunity of a lifetime here. Not many kids from where I grew up get an Ivy League education—in fact, ninety-nine percent of them don't. Maybe I am spoiled? Maybe Evan can see right through me? It's easier to think that's the reason he walked away, rather than think he was disgusted by my feelings for him. I know Evan isn't hateful, but a lot of time has passed since we were neighbors. Who knows what has happened to make him jaded? Who knows what new opinions he's formed? Even if he's fine with me being bi, finding out your best friend for all those years had secret romantic feelings for you must be disorienting.

By the time Priestley and the other guys show up, I've composed myself enough to smile and act like everything's fine.

We go out onto the court to meet Harvard in the next match of the Ivy League. This is the last tournament before regionals, and after that, we break for summer. I try not to imagine a whole summer without school and tennis to keep me occupied. Whatever vacation my mom and Bryce have planned. Since I was fifteen, we've been going on incredible vacations: skiing in Aspen, a cruise around the Mediterranean, driving sports cars down the Amalfi Coast. It makes my fists clench now just thinking about it. What was Evan doing while we were galivanting around Europe? Taking care of his sick dad and working long hours for minimum wage? Was he thinking about me? Did he miss me at all?

Priestley slaps me on the back and I snap out of it.

"You ready for this, Carter?"

I nod, force myself to smile.

After Ben and Miles win the first doubles point, it's time for Priestley and me to go out there and do our thing. I'm a little tight at first, but luckily, Priestley carries us until I can loosen up and get into a rhythm. When it's my turn to serve, I take a deep breath and allow the sounds of the court to wash over me. Birds chirping in nearby trees. My teammates' tennis shoes shuffling on the hardcourt while they anxiously await the ball toss. And then the bounce of the ball, the rush of air as I bring the racket down.

I serve an ace, winning a genuine smile from Priestley. He pulls me in as we slap hands.

"You had me nervous for a second there, Carter."

I swallow and force the smile to remain on my face. "Don't worry, I was just warming up."

We win our doubles point and end up thrashing Harvard in a shut-out. Even Priestley is in a good enough mood to agree to drinks at the student bar to celebrate.

We're two beers in when my phone buzzes with a call.

I take it out of my pocket to see who it is, expecting my mom or Bryce. When I see the name on the screen, my heart lurches into my throat.

I rush outside to answer it.

"Hello? Evan?"

"I'm at the beach," he says before hanging up.

10

EVAN

I wait for another wave before I walk into the sea. The water's so cold when it washes over me, it takes my breath away, makes it feel like I'll never be able to catch my breath again, just for a second.

Everything is blank as the water consumes me. It roars in my ears and I gulp in water and start to choke.

My lungs burn and my legs carry me out of the water.

"Yo man, what are you doing out there?" Adam shouts from the shore.

"You're a crazy motherfucker." Paddy laughs.

I shake myself dry, making sure to splash Paddy in the face.

"Why are we sitting round here, anyway?" Adam asks.

"You guys wanna get high?"

Adam bites his lip. Paddy's eyes light up. Corey looks up from where he'd been drawing lines in the sand with a stick.

We go into the woods to smoke, not coming out until it's dark. The moon hides behind a sky full of dark clouds. I shiver in my t-shirt. The weed hasn't done enough to numb me.

The guys laugh at stupid shit. Push each other into strangers on the boardwalk who are too scared of them to say shit.

A couple walk towards us arm-in-arm, the woman leaning in to say something in the guy's ear. My stomach drops and I feel like pushing them. Feel like tearing something apart.

We duck into an arcade and I put some coins in the punchbag machine and have at it, taking my frustration out on that instead of someone's face.

I don't wanna think. I can't.

What the fuck did Nate think he was doing telling me that shit?

Telling me had some sort of crush on me?

Dangling shit in front of my face I can't have.

Adam picks up a couple of girls standing by the water ice stand. One of them keeps smiling at me and flipping her hair and Adam keeps elbowing me in the ribs. Panic rises up when she sidles in close, her sweet perfume in my nostrils, the smell of Cherry Coke on her breath when she leans in to tell me her name.

I barely hear it. "I've gotta go."

I don't wait for their reactions, I've just got to get out of here.

I can't go home. Ma might be up and I can't see her like this. Can't let her smell the weed on me.

I head back toward the beach. The sound of the sea calling me over. The sand rough on the soles of my feet when I take my shoes off. The ground getting wet, soggy, squelching between my toes.

I take in a deep inhale, smell the salt water, the stink of fish and seaweed washed up on the shore. Nate's face surfaces in my mind. His big Bambi eyes when I told him I had to go. How fucking vulnerable he looked telling me that shit. I wanna be mad at him, but I'm not.

I take my phone out, just to look at his name in my contacts. Nate fucking Castellani. Or is it something else now? I hit call, sure the roar of the waves will wash out his voice, but I can hear it. Clear as fucking day. Nate, saying my name.

I put the phone to my ear. "I'm at the beach," I say before hanging up.

I'm so fucking tired. I clench my teeth and sit down on the sand, pulling my knees into my chest.

A calm washes over me as I sit and watch the black water, waiting for Nate. I know he'll come. And that's what fucking scares me. How quick that trust came back. Even that niggling voice in the back of my head telling me he'll leave again is quiet while I sit there. But I can't push down that giddiness at the knowledge that Nate wanted me back then. All those years, it wasn't just a one-way thing.

The tires of a big car crunch on the gravel lining the beach, but I don't turn around. I don't even turn my head until he's sitting right next to me. His smell overtaking the smell of seaweed and salt. Warmth coming off him in waves.

When I look at him, he's looking at the sea, his face tense.

"Sorry I was a dick before." My voice comes out sounding weird, like it doesn't belong to me.

"It's okay." He shakes his head.

"It's not."

He stays quiet. Hands clasped over his knees. He's wearing one of those backward caps. A polo shirt and chinos. Nikes so white they glow in the dark.

"You can't just say shit like that."

"Why not?" He looks at me and I look away.

"Because ... you're you and I'm me."

"What does that mean?"

"It means ... you're not the boy next door anymore. I'm staying here, forever, I'm not goin' anywhere."

He blinks, frowns. "Does this mean you're not mad I told you I'm bi, that I had a crush on you?"

Had? My stomach drops. I didn't realize how much I was hoping that crush still stood until he told me it was in the past.

"No, I'm not mad about that."

I swallow, force myself to say it. To tell him the truth. "I've been with guys, like that."

His head snaps in my direction.

"A lot of guys," I add.

"Oh."

I throw him a challenging look, but I can't meet his gaze.

"What was ... " He shuffles, his chinos making a shuffling sound against the sand. "What was it like?"

Was that curiosity in his voice? Jealousy? Desire? It kills me that I can't read him like I used to be able to.

"It was ... " I shrug. "It made me forget."

"Forget what?"

"Everything. Shit with my dad, my ma, being here, never getting out, everything."

I hear him swallow over the sound of the sea.

"Is that why you did it? To forget?"

"I guess. That was one reason."

"What's the other?"

"Because it felt good."

His breath hitches and my dick twitches. Not Nate. Not this, with him. But I want it. I fucking want it, more than I've ever wanted anything.

"I've only ever been with girls," he says. "I liked it. But ...

I've thought about you. A lot. But not for a while. And then ... now we've been spending time together...."

Still? My heart races and I try to still the thoughts rushing to the forefront.

"I watched gay porn yesterday."

I snort. He's such a fucking dork. Too innocent. "For the first time?"

"Yeah."

"How was it?"

"Stupid?" He shrugs. "Hot as fuck."

"Did you jerk off?" I swallow, heat pooling in the pit of my stomach.

"Yeah."

When I look at his face, his cheeks are bright red.

"Why'd you come back, Nate?" I ask, more softly this time.

"I told you. I missed you."

"It can't be like it was when we were kids."

"I know that. But maybe it could be ... better?"

Nothing could be better than being a kid with Nate. Feeling like you'll never be alone a second of your life.

I stand up and take my shirt off. The weed's wearing off properly now and I feel like I wanna crawl out of my skin. Like everything's too raw and real and too much.

Nate doesn't move at first and I slip out of my sweats and head down to the water.

It isn't until I've ducked my head under and come back up that he starts to follow. His body in his white Calvin Kleins makes every part of me ache. I've never been with someone who looks like Nate before. Never felt like I deserved someone like him.

He ducks his head under and comes back up, looking at me. The moonlight flitting through the clouds, making slashes on his tanned skin. His dark hair plastered across his forehead.

He's shivering when he puts his hand out and I look at it, mind racing.

"Evan," he says and I take it, letting him pull me towards him.

His skin starts to warm up when I press against it. His breath is hot on the side of my face. He's hard under his boxers. He puts his arms around me and just holds me. His hand on the back of my neck, stroking. I press my lips against his skin. It's salty with sweat and sea water. I brush my lips up his neck and feel him shiver. He grinds his cock against mine and tightens his grip around my waist.

I pull back enough to catch his lips. Don't stop to ask myself what the fuck I'm doing. This is *Nate,* for fuck sake.

But he's kissing me back, holding me so tight I don't think I could escape even if I wanted to.

We kiss like it's the first time we've ever kissed anyone. Just exploring, not even using tongue. Nate brushes his lips across my mouth, his breath between my lips. I open my eyes and he's right there.

"Remember when we used to press our faces up close like this," he whispers. "When we'd pretend to be cyclops?"

I brush his hair out of his face.

"You're ruining the moment," I say, but I haven't moved my face. And he hasn't stopped pressing his body, his hard-on, against me. If it was ever gonna be anything with Nate, it was gonna be like this. Laughing and remembering stupid shit. Not like it is with those random guys in the woods.

He presses his mouth to my neck and starts kissing down to my collarbone. Brushing his lips against my skin while he sighs. I run my hand through his wet hair, watching his head where it's cradled in my arm.

"Let's get out of the water."

"Why?"

"Because it's cold and everyone can see us here."

He looks up, back at the sand, but he doesn't look worried. "There's no one around."

"But someone *could* see us."

He loosens his grip enough for me to start wading back to shore. I can hear him behind me, his body pushing through the water.

It's cold now and we're gonna be covered in sand if we sit down in our wet underwear. I take his hand and lead him to the wall of showers where people rinse their dogs and kids off and get the sand off their feet before putting on their shoes. We used to play in these showers until we were prunes. Splash each other and fill up water balloons. Trying to be fast before the lifeguard caught us.

I never imagined I'd be standing under them with him like this, not even trying to hide how hard we are for each other.

He lets me rinse him off. The water is lukewarm, but it takes the bite out of the air.

Nate leans in and kisses me again, this time exploring with his tongue. His abs press against me. His skin smooth and warm.

I splay my hand across his bare chest, pressing him back against the wall. He gasps the second I touch him. His cock is fighting to get out of his boxers. I slide my hand down to his waistband and pull until he springs free.

He watches me the whole time. Those trusting fucking Bambi eyes on me.

He pushes his hips off the wall so I can pull his underwear down to his knees. I wipe my hand on my chest, just in case there's any lingering sand, before spitting into my palm and gripping the base of his cock.

He gasps again, this time louder, more desperate. His hips buck into my hand.

He runs his hand up and down my arm while I jerk him off, trying not to look him in the eye.

"Evan."

Fuck.

"Evan, look at me."

The second I do, I lose control. Let him pull me closer until I'm flush against him. Kissing him, taking his tongue in my mouth, his moan vibrating through me.

He pushes my hand away and opens his legs, kicking his underwear down past his knees so he can pull me between his thighs.

The water trickles over us as we kiss and grind against each other. Nate is trying to pull my boxers off, the water making them cling to my skin, and I'm not helping him.

"Please," he says. "Evan, take these off, I need you to be naked."

I stop long enough to pull my boxers down to my knees. "I knew you'd be fucking bossy."

He lets out a breath of a laugh.

"Shut up and kiss me again."

Nate grips my ass while I grind against him. We need lube. Nate deserves a bed, someone better than me. But that selfish part of my brain that wants this more than anything won't stop. Not unless he asks me to. And he's definitely not doing that.

If anything, he's pulling me closer with his legs while he digs his fingers into my ass-cheeks.

I take my hand back and lick the palm before I slide it between our bodies and take Nate in my grip again. He goes stiff as I pump his cock. He throws his head back, closing his eyes. His mouth open as he pants in time to my movements. I watch him. His fucking beautiful face. Trusting me.

Pre-cum beads on his slit and I use my thumb to smear it down his shaft. He moans, eyes shooting open on a gasp, and I was right. He looks surprised the second before he shoots his load all over us, eyes rolling back in his head.

My heart pounds as I milk the last of it from him, resisting the urge to slide down his body and lick him clean.

He looks at me, all Bambi eyes again. Vulnerable and on display. Trusting. So fucking stupidly trusting.

"Okay?"

He nods, licks his lips and smiles. His hand sliding down my stomach before I pull away. "You don't have to do that."

"I want to."

But I've turned away from him now, pulling my boxers up with the hand that isn't covered in Nate's cum.

"Evan, I-"

He stops talking as I wash him off. Being gentler with him than I've ever been with anyone I've fucked. I can't look at him as I wash cum from his belly, but I can feel his eyes on me as I do it and my face flushes hot the whole time.

I wait for the moment of regret as we slip back into our clothes. The shame. But it doesn't come.

"If you don't get in my car, I'm gonna be really mad," he says.

"Fine, I'll get in your car. But only if you promise not to play that emo shit."

He tuts. "I thought you liked that emo shit."

"Since when?"

He smiles, shaking his head.

The car still smells like pine trees, and after a while, our bodies. Salt water and Nate's sweat and cum.

My cock is still hard under my damp underwear, but I'm not frustrated. I don't need to take care of it. Not yet. I can't stop looking at my hand. Thinking about Nate spilling through my fingers. His face when he came. When I made him come.

The lights are off when we reach the house. He stops the car and puts his hand on my knee when I try to get out.

"Wait."

"Don't worry," I say before he can say anything to ruin it. "We're cool."

He swallows and nods. "Okay."

I open the car door.

"Evan?"

"Yeah?"

"You'll call me, right?"

When did anyone not call Nate after a hookup? Just the sight of him, looking all clean in his nice clothes, in his nice car, with his perfect skin and sexily messy hair. His cheeks all pink from getting a hand job under a shower. His conventionally handsome face and frat boy body. You don't need to be a genius to know this guy has never had problems getting dates.

"Yeah, I'll call you."

The house is quiet when I let myself in. I tiptoe upstairs and get into bed, still so hard it hurts. But I refuse to touch myself. As if leaving it will make what happened that much different. Make it just for him.

11

NATHAN

The frat house was quiet when I got home last night. I was still in a daze as I let myself in and walked up the stairs to the shower. Peeling my damp clothes off my body. Remembering Evan hovering over me, making me feel good.

When I climbed into bed, I thought about all the other stuff too, like how Evan said he'd been with men, a lot of men. In the moment, it excited me, because it meant he might want to be with me. That he might not be as out of reach as I'd always thought.

But lying there in bed, replaying his words, the jealousy surfaces. Thinking about Evan touching all those other men the way he touched me. Them touching him. Probably making him feel better than I ever could.

His words came back—*because it feels good.*

Could I ever make him feel the way those men have?

EVERYONE'S up when I come downstairs, Ben manning the blender as usual. Priestley's at the coffee machine, drinking an espresso with his hair perfectly coiffed and the collar popped on his polo, looking like he's been up for hours.

He raises an eyebrow at my appearance. I'm still wearing the ratty t-shirt and shorts I slept in last night. When I run a hand through my hair, it's a mess and I can smell myself.

"Late night, Carter?" Priestley asks.

Ben flashes me a look I can't read, but I'm sure he looks sad. Did something happen while I was away last night?

I ignore Priestley, taking a glass of green goop from the counter and forcing some down.

"*Gah*, what's in this?"

Ben takes a beat before replying. "Celery, kale, coconut water...."

I don't need to hear another word. I leave the glass on the counter and open the fridge, looking for something edible.

Priestley eyes me suspiciously as I reach for some cold pizza. "Don't you understand that we're supposed to be in the best shape of our lives right now? Regionals are only a few months away-"

"I know, don't worry. I'm in good shape."

His eyes scan my body in my sleep clothes and I feel exposed, like the dude has x-ray vision or something. I resist the urge to cover up.

PRIESTLEY SOMEHOW MANAGES TO 'ENCOURAGE' me to gulp down one of Ben's disgusting 'smoothies' before we leave for practice.

I still feel a little sick when we get to the locker room and start changing into our tennis clothes.

Even after four years of private school, the second I stepped into this room, I felt like an intruder. Like someone

—someone like Priestley Rosenthal—was going to see me and point me out as the imposter.

But it never happened. I'm still here. These crisp, navy tennis clothes with the logo of an Ivy League college belong to me. That's my name on my cubby. My Wilson rackets neatly lined up. My custom tennis shoes. At some point, I stopped being intimidated.

I'm smiling to myself at the memory of last night when I catch Ben watching me. He's biting the inside of his lip like he does sometimes when he's nervous or something's bothering him. I'm about to ask him what's wrong when Coach comes in and asks us if we're ready.

We get out onto the courts. Do our warmups. Everyone is super focused and Coach keeps reminding us about regionals. How important they are. What an incredible opportunity it is to be seen by pro coaches and trainers. People who can help us break into the ATP. I let this go over my head. I'll never break into the ATP, but I do want to take us to regionals and make our coaches proud.

After practice, I make a beeline for Ben and ask him to study with me at the library. I need to get him alone and find out what's wrong. If it's Priestley, I'm going to have to put my big boy pants on and talk to him as his VP, tell him that bullying is not acceptable. That his leadership style doesn't work with everyone. It'll be good practice for the real world —as Bryce keeps reminding me. When I'll have to deal with all kinds of personalities.

We find a table in a reasonably quiet spot in the library and Ben starts taking his books out of his bag.

"Hey, Ben, can I ask you something?"

He looks up, his eyes all big and worried. Ben has such a babyface, it's easy to forget he's my age and can probably take care of himself. Something about him just brings out that protective instinct in me. One I've never actually been much good with, seeing as there was always someone to look out for me—like my mom, or Evan's parents, or Bryce, or Evan himself.

"Is everything okay with you? You seem ... a little down. Did Priestley do something when I was out last night?"

He frowns, looking confused. Either I'm completely off-base or he's a really good actor. I don't think it's the latter. He flushes before looking down and making a big fuss getting his laptop out of his backpack.

"Ben, what is it?"

He drags his teeth over his bottom lip and my stomach does summersaults as I wait for him to tell me what's wrong.

"Were you out with that guy last night?"

Okay, I wasn't expecting that. Is he mad about me seeing Evan?

"Yeah, why?"

He swallows, looks down, shakes his head. "Nothing, it doesn't matter."

He takes his laptop out and opens it on the desk.

"Ben, do you have a problem with me being bi?"

"What? No, of course not." His face heats up.

"Tell me, what is it? I'm not letting it drop until you tell me."

"It's just ... I wish you would have told me earlier, about being bi."

I frown. "What difference does it make? I wasn't even sure I was ... " my stomach drops. "Why? Would you have not been my friend if you'd known I'm not straight?"

"What?" His voice comes out strangled. "Of course not, I'm not a homophobe, Nate. Jesus."

Now I flush. "So what then?"

He takes a deep breath. "It's because ... it might have

been easier to talk to you about ... well ... I'm, I think ... No, I know I'm gay."

I blink. Am I really so clueless and self-involved that I missed the fact that two of my best friends are gay?

"Say something."

"I ... well obviously it's fine. I mean, I support you." I run a hand over my face. "I'm sorry you felt like you couldn't tell me."

"I ... I didn't think you were a bigot or anything, I just ... needed to figure some things out myself first."

"So have you been with a guy?"

He shakes his head. "I haven't been with anyone."

I try not to react to that the way my instincts want me to. Ben has a babyface, but he's still adorable. I would have expected him to at least have experience with a girl or two. I've definitely seen girls flirting with him at parties. I just thought he was shy. Now it all makes sense.

"Do you want to?"

"Yes, but not right this minute."

"Why not?"

His face flushes again. "I want to focus on our thing. On our business idea and school and tennis and everything."

I think about how distracted this thing with Evan has made me. It makes sense. If I was smarter, I'd probably copy Ben—but I know myself well enough to know that I couldn't stop pursuing Evan now.

"What about you and this guy? Did something happen last night?"

"Yeah. We hooked up a little."

"Oh."

Why does he still seem sad?

"You know you can hook up with guys without it being a

big thing, right? It doesn't have to get in the way of school and tennis and our thing?"

"I know. I just don't want to."

"Okay." I want to push, but I drop it for now. The last thing I want to do is make him regret opening up to me.

"So what's happening with you and Evan now? Are you in a relationship?"

"I don't know. He's going through a lot at the minute. I don't want to rush him. His dad just died and ... we're working through things. A lot of shit happened in the past, a lot of shit I didn't even know about."

"You mean all the stuff with Bryce?"

I nod.

"Are you going to speak to Bryce about it?"

My stomach churns at the thought of trying to call my stepdad out. I've never done anything like that before. I've never wanted to cause any more trouble than I already have for my mom. "It's in the past. And I'm pissed at him, sure. But I imagine he was just doing what he thought was best for me. He didn't even know Evan."

TALKING to Ben has made me want answers. I meant what I said back at the library, I understand that Evan's going through a hard time, and I'd never want to rush him into anything, but I would like to know that he at least feels the same way I do. That last night wasn't just a hookup.

I send a text, asking what he's up to. I don't get a reply straight away. The more I stare at my phone, the more silent it seems to be.

When I do finally get a reply, it's short and almost curt.

I'm working tonight.

My heart drops. I want to see him again so bad it's a physical ache.

I draft my reply three times before finally hitting send.

Ok cool, can I see you after?

Someone knocks on my bedroom door.

"What?" I bark.

The door cracks open as if I'd said *come in*. "Did I catch you at a bad time?" Priestley asks.

"No, I was just...."

"Who are you texting? Is it this mystery girl who made you late for practice?"

I keep my mouth shut, not knowing what to say.

My phone buzzes with a reply and I have to stop myself from pouncing on it.

Priestley cocks his head. "Aren't you going to answer that?"

I shake my head.

He laughs. "Why all the secrecy? Is it Mira? Is that it?"

"What? No. Of course it's not Mira. Mira's with Mark."

He cocks an eyebrow. "Exactly."

"No, Mira's not cheating on Mark. It's not her."

"Okay, so why the secrecy? If you really like this girl, why don't you bring her to the next mixer? We can all meet her."

"Um."

"Unless it's just a hookup?"

I instantly prickle. Evan is not a 'just a hookup.' "What if it's not a girl?"

"What?"

"I said, what if it's a guy I'm texting?"

He shrugs. "So, you're telling me you're gay?"

"Bi."

"Fine. Why wouldn't you just tell me that in the first place? Do you think I'm some kind of small-minded bigot?"

I just blink at him before spluttering a reply. "No, I just-"

"You do know my little brother is gay, right? Not that that's the reason I don't care, but, you know, maybe if you paid more attention to other people, you wouldn't get so wrapped up in your own head."

Shit. Am I really that self-involved? I didn't know Evan was gay. Didn't know Ben was gay. I'm about to apologize when I notice Priestley is smirking. I've never even met his family.

"What the fuck Priestley? Why would I know your little brother's gay?"

He chuckles.

"You're such a dick sometimes."

He gets serious in 0.2 seconds flat. "Nathan, I don't care who you sleep with, so long as it doesn't affect your work here or out on the court, okay?"

I nod, feeling like a little kid being chastised.

He leaves, closing the door behind him and I pounce on my phone to see Evan's reply.

I don't finish till 11

That's ok

I wait for a reply, staring at the phone.

You know the warehouse off Applegate?
Behind the golf course?

I know it, I'll see you there.

I consider putting some sort of emoji on the end, like a kissy face or something, but decide against it at the last second.

I've got hours until I can meet Evan. It gives me more than enough time to imagine what's going to happen when the time comes. I'll be happy to do exactly what we did last night, only this time, I want to repay the favor. Watch Evan come apart for me. Watch that wall he's built up over the past five years melt away.

I leave a half hour early and sit outside the warehouse in my car. I couldn't decide on a playlist to listen to so I just have the radio playing quietly in the background. I'm not listening to it anyway.

The second I see people start to leave the building, I sit forward in my seat, then realize I should try and look natural and relax.

Evan comes out after a group of tired-looking guys in beanies and big coats. It's warm out, but it must be cold in the warehouse.

Evan's wearing a bubble coat, no hat, his shaved head on display. A pair of slouchy work pants and bulky black boots.

A fire burns in the pit of my stomach at the sight of him. I'm suddenly ashamed of my pine-scented SUV. The labels in my clothes. The cleanness of my sneakers. The fact I've never done a day's hard labor in my life outside of shirtless charity car washes on Greek Row.

Evan's gaze flickers to mine quickly before flickering away again.

He opens the passenger side door and climbs in.

"Hey."

"Hey."

"Shall we go to your place?"

"No. My ma's there."

"I know that, but your mom likes me." I try for a charming smile, but Evan isn't even looking at me.

"I thought you wanted to...." he trails off.

"I do," I reply in a small voice. "But I wanna hang out with you too."

He glances at the backseat.

"Drive down West Ave. I know a place."

My mouth is dry as I start the car. This isn't what I want. Is it? Not like this. I drive anyway, doing as he says. He's quiet, like he's a stranger. If I'd thought what happened between us would bring us closer, I couldn't have been more wrong.

The radio is mostly talking now. Neither of us are listening. My leg bouncing nervously while I drive. Evan's completely still, like he's checked out.

The river's coming up on our right. The big houses surrounding the golf course and those big tanks of oil we used to make stories up about when we were kids.

I stop the car behind a pickup truck, a security gate with barbed wire surrounding a construction site.

"Not here," Evan says. "A little farther up."

"Evan, we should talk."

He won't look at me.

"I don't want it like this, not with you."

"What are you talking about?"

"I don't want to fuck in the back of my car."

He looks at me now, his eyes are dark, like he's hidden from me.

"Why not? You were okay with it on the beach."

"That just happened. Ev, I don't know what's going on here, and I'm confused as hell, but I know that this feels wrong. I'd rather go home and talk. You're completely checked out from me right now and I hate it."

He clenches his jaw. I think he's going to snap, say something, tell me I don't belong here anymore, or I don't know who he is now.

His eyes soften. He sinks back into the chair.

"We can't go to my place. It's late, we'll wake my ma and Stacie up."

"Okay, so let's stay here, let's talk."

"About what?"

I unfasten my seatbelt. "About anything." I shrug.

He looks straight ahead, out of the windshield, his seatbelt still firmly in place.

"Tell me about what you said on the beach."

"Which part?"

"The men."

His jaw clenches again. "No."

"Why not?"

He just shakes his head.

"Okay, so let's talk about your dad."

"Jesus Christ, Nate."

"What?"

"No, not that."

"Okay. I'm sorry."

"Don't ... " He runs a hand over his face. "Don't apologize, just ... lay off a little, yeah?"

"Okay."

"Why don't you tell me something?" he says.

"Shoot."

"Since when were you into guys?"

"I told you, I'm only into you."

He snorts, finally looking at me. "That's not a thing."

I shrug. "What do you want me to tell you? I'm not going to lie. I've never looked at another guy the way I look at you."

He glances down at his legs in his work pants, a frown ghosting his face. If he asks me why, I don't know what I'll say.

"You told me you watched gay porn and got off to it," he says instead. "So you must be into guys other than me."

"That was just sex."

"So was what I did with those guys."

"But not me?"

He doesn't answer.

"Did you think about me like that when we were growing up together?"

One side of his mouth twitches in a smile. "I might have rubbed one or two out over you, sure."

My cock twitches under my chinos.

When he looks at me I think I'm going to melt.

"Me too," I practically whisper.

He licks his lips. "Sure you don't wanna fuck in the back of your car?"

I reach across the gearstick and put my hand over his.

"I told you, not here," he says.

"No, listen, my mom and Bryce are going to the Bahamas. I've got tennis matches all weekend. But after that, maybe you could come over."

My face is so hot, I think it's going to set on fire. I can hear Evan breathing in the confined space of the car. I catch the scent coming off his work clothes. Something unfamiliar. It's a cold smell and reminds me of sawdust and damp cardboard. He wraps his fingers around mine.

"Maybe."

When I look up, he's smiling.

I lean in and kiss him. He lets me, for a minute, before pulling away.

"They've got cameras here."

"So what? We're not doing anything illegal."

"Actually, you shouldn't be parked here."

"What are you? The traffic police?"

"Nate Castellani's a badass now."

I love the way my name sounds coming from his mouth —my real name.

I can't stop myself from kissing him again. I trace the shape of his lips with mine. That bow shape his top lip makes. I can taste cigarettes and coffee on his tongue. And I can feel his hunger in the kiss. In the way he puts his hand on the back of my head and keeps me there, fingers gripping my hair.

I'm breathless when I pull away. "We should have done this years ago."

"Nah."

"Why not?"

"Because, I would have been even more pissed when you moved away."

"I'm sor-"

"Shut the fuck up, Nate." He kisses me to stop me from saying anything stupid.

The kiss gets more heated, until he's guiding me over the gearstick into his lap. It's a tight squeeze, my ass pressed against the dashboard.

"I thought you said-"

"Shut up, Nate."

I grind against him, feeling how hard he is under his work pants.

He pulls away.

"You're gonna drive to the place and we're gonna give each other a hand job exactly like this, okay?"

I nod.

"No one's fucking in your backseat. Is that a good compromise?"

"That sounds reasonable."

He smirks, giving my ass a squeeze through my chinos.

"Hurry up."

I climb awkwardly back into the driver's seat, banging my knee on the dashboard.

Evan's running his hand over his head while I back out from behind the pickup truck.

The spot he tells me to park at is under the cover of a patch of trees by the jetty.

"Sure there's no cameras here?"

"I'm sure."

I wish I hadn't asked when I realize how he knows this. How many men has he been with here and places like it? I remind myself I have no right to be jealous. I wasn't there.

This time, when I switch off the engine, he unclicks his belt and waits for me to climb into his lap.

It feels wild, but not weird. I've never done anything like this in a car before. Mira would have hit me with her purse if I tried to get fresh with her anywhere other than her dorm room.

I feel completely out of control. Even if I'm the one driving the situation. Evan's trapped under my body, letting me grind against him. His hands coming from my hips to my ass as he pushes his hips up to meet mine.

I kiss him, hard and desperate, gripping the back of the headrest while I grind my cock against his.

Evan pulls back with some effort.

"Fuck, Nate."

He grips my hard-on through my chinos and I whine. Evan's lips find my neck as he unzips my pants, sliding his hand under the fabric, his fingertips stroking over the wet patch in my boxer briefs. I groan against his neck while I grind against him.

He guides me up, my feet finding purchase on the side of the seat so Evan can pull my pants and underwear down.

I know he's seen my cock, last night on the beach. He watched me come all over myself. But this feels different. The light from the dashboard and the jetty expose me more than the moonlight on the beach did. I know he must be able to smell me the way I smell him, without the masking of salt water and sand and musty seaweed.

I almost pull a muscle trying to get my pants down past my knees.

"*Argh, fuck*. I can't get them off."

Evan laughs. "You're gonna have to start wearing skirts with nothing underneath."

My face flushes.

"I'm just kidding, Nate."

"Can we get out?"

I start pulling my pants up and he gets the wrong idea.

"Yeah, sure, we don't have to-"

"I don't mean that, I just want more space, with you. I wanna get naked with you."

"It's not warm enough to do that."

I ignore him, opening the door once my pants are all the way back up.

There's a breeze coming off the river, but it's not freezing.

I pull him over to a tree by the coat, kissing him, feeling drunk on him.

My pants are still open. He pulls them down, tugging them over my ass and then down past my knees. My cock springs to attention.

Evan drops to his knees, looking up at me before taking the head of my cock into his mouth.

"Fuck!" I throw my head back and grip the back of his.

He doesn't stop until I'm buried in his throat.

"Oh fuck, Evan, how are you so good at...." he swallows around me and I almost lose it. "Stop!"

He pulls off and looks up at me, rubbing my hip. "What's wrong?"

"Come back."

When he stands up, I grab him and kiss him, his lips swollen and hot. I'm frantic as I reach for his fly, unzipping his work pants, tugging the stiff fabric until it's under his ass. I grip his bare cheeks, wanting every part of him. Exploring parts of Evan's body I'd always wanted to touch, but never been allowed to have before.

His spit on my cock transfers onto his as we grind. Evan groaning into my mouth. I slide my hand up his shirt and stroke his stomach, his back and pecs and collarbones. Ghosting over his nipples, feeling them pebble harder under my touch.

He groans against my neck, brushing his lips over the clammy skin, licking behind my ear.

"Please," I whisper.

"Tell me what you want, Nate."

"You." I slide my hand up the back of his shirt until I'm gripping between his shoulder-blades, feeling the muscles under his skin flex with his movements. "I want all of you."

He spins us until his back is pinned against the tree. I keep kissing him, the sound of rustling in his pocket. When he pulls away, he's holding a condom.

My heart races. He wants to fuck me. Am I ready for that? Right now, I'd let Evan do whatever he wants to me.

"Put it on."

On *me,* right.

I take it, my hands trembling. He takes it back.

"I'll do it."

"Are you sure?"

Him tearing into the condom wrapper is answer enough.

I shiver when he slides the latex over the head of my cock, rolling it down slowly until he reaches the base.

He grips the back of my neck and makes me look at him. "Good?"

I nod. I don't think I can talk right now.

He reaches back into his pocket and pulls out a sachet, tearing into it with his teeth. He takes my hand and squeezes lube out into it.

"Get me ready, then fuck me."

Holy fuck, Evan wants me to fuck him.

I nod dumbly as he turns to face the tree. The pale skin beyond the tan lines glowing under the lights in the jetty. I grip one cheek with my clean hand and he groans. Before I can even think about it, I'm on my knees, kissing the smooth skin covering his ass, lapping up the sound of his sighs. I brush my lips across his skin, moving slowly to his crack. Feathering kisses to that spot at the base of his spine where two thumb-shaped dents sit. I'm going to put my thumbs in those dents. I'm going to make Evan feel good if it's the last thing I do.

I separate his cheeks and he opens his legs wider to let me in. He's trusting me. And that trust, it feels better than any fuck ever could.

I lick a stripe up his crack and he shivers under my touch.

"*Fuck*, Nate."

That video I watched, how much it turned me on, surfaces in my mind and I let go. Plunging my tongue between his cheeks, searching until I find his warm, tight hole. I prod and am let in an inch. Evan makes a noise, something between a grunt and a moan. My cock aches at the knowledge I'm making him feel this good.

His breaths become pants when I start to fuck him with

my tongue. The sensation of his hole tightening around me makes my cock stand to attention, impatiently waiting its turn. I tell it to hold on, because, I could do this for hours if Evan would let me. But we are technically in public here.

I force myself to stop and replace my tongue with my fingers. Evan's knees are bent, his legs open. He starts to push back on my fingers, opening up for me.

"Now," he growls.

I stand up and press a kiss to the back of his neck. His shirt's soaked through with sweat. I push it up so I can get better access to him, sliding my own polo up and pressing my bare chest against his back. The contact of skin on skin is electric. I slide my hand down the front of his body and use the lube to stroke his cock. He's rock hard, pre-cum beading on the tip.

"*Fuck*, Nate, do it now."

I line the head of my cock up, sliding it between his cheeks, feeling his hole right there, tight and hot and waiting for me. My head pushes in and Evan's body tightens around me.

"Oh, *fuck*." My head falls on his shoulder.

"That's it, Nate."

He reaches around and guides me by the hip, pulling me deeper until I bottom out.

We both gasp and stop moving.

"Okay?" I ask.

"Yeah."

I gives his cock another stroke and moans, letting his head drop back onto my shoulder. Giving me access to his neck. I take advantage, kissing and licking the smooth, tan skin on display.

I pull out a little before slowly thrusting back in. Evan's moans tell me I'm doing something right.

His head drops forward, his forehead resting on the tree.

I move slow at first. Evan starts pushing back in time with my thrusts until we find a rhythm and speed up. I try not to get too much in my head. Think about the fact I'm fucking Evan. *My* Evan.

Our moans and grunts are in-sync with our thrusts. I could stay in this moment forever. Evan's half naked body glowing under the jetty lights, shivering under my touch, pleasure rippling through it because I'm inside him.

He grips his cock and pushes back faster, harder, our skin slapping in the silence. "Now, *fuck*, I'm gonna come."

I keep up with his thrusts, gripping his hips tight as the tingle and heat build in the pit of my stomach. His muscles tighten around me, impossibly, contracting, pulsing as a deep, throaty moan rips through him. The sensation of his body clamping around me and the knowledge I made him come sends me over the edge.

I say his name over and over as I spill into the condom, his body growing limp in my hands.

I need a few seconds to recover. My cock pulsing inside him. He shudders and pulls away and I grip the base of the condom to make sure I don't lose it as I pull out.

Evan pulls his pants up, his shirt falling down in the process.

When he turns, his face is red, sweat beading on his forehead and top lip. I can see him trying to escape, now that the moment's over, but I won't let him. I pull him in by the neck and kiss him.

"That was amazing." I say.

He smiles but he won't look at me.

I give him a lazy smile and flinch when he snaps the condom off my twitching cock before tucking my dick back in my pants for me.

"Thank you."

He laughs, shaking his head, tying a knot in the condom before tossing it into the trees.

"You shouldn't do that."

"Do you have a trash can on you?"

I shake my head. I can feel him watching me. Feel the curiosity and confusion coming from him.

"We should go, before someone comes out here an catches us."

"I thought it was safe here?"

"It is, but you were so loud, I wouldn't be surprised if people in Brooklyn heard."

"*I* was loud?"

"Fuck you." He laughs.

I didn't think it was possible to be *us* in this situation. I just fucked my best friend, and it felt like the most natural thing in the world. He's still him and I'm still me. We're still *us.*

When he gets back in the car, Evan rests his head against the headrest. I put a playlist on my phone.

He registers what's playing—*Demolition Lovers* by My Chemical Romance.

"Not this emo shit." He laughs, shaking his head.

"Do you wanna choose?"

I toss my phone into his lap, but he just leaves it there, letting the song play.

12

EVAN

As I let myself into the house after Nate drops me off, I try to tell myself it was just like the other times. Nate just wanted my ass like those guys I meet online. But I can't even fool myself. It wasn't like the other times. And Nate wanted more than a quick fuck. When I tried to take him to that place, he stopped the car and told me he didn't wanna fuck me on the backseat.

It was probably still the stupidest thing I've ever done. Now, this time, when he leaves, it's gonna suck even worse. I'm gonna hate him even more.

When I get up the next morning, Ma's at the counter in her work clothes, spreading peanut butter on bread.

"You were out late last night," she says.

I open the fridge, get the OJ out and swig it from the carton.

"I heard you come home around three. What were you doing out that late?"

There's a hint of worry in her voice and I don't wanna be the cause of that.

"I was out with Nate."

"Nate? At that time?" She puts the knife down and turns to give me her full attention.

Don't blush. Don't let her see what you're hiding.

I shrug. "I thought you wanted me to hang out with him?"

"I do, it's just ... I didn't think Nate would-"

"What? Good boy Nate doesn't stay out past curfew?"

She shakes her head. "What were you two even doing out that late?"

I turn my back so she can't see my face heat up.

"Talking."

She pauses. "Talking? About what?"

"Just stuff." I shrug.

When I turn back around, she's still standing there, staring at me. "It's good I guess, you having someone to talk to." She shakes her head and picks the knife up again. "Nate won't get in trouble for staying out late?"

"He's a big boy, Ma."

My cock twitches at the memory of how much of a big boy Nate is.

"He can take care of himself."

"I know that."

"Are you worried I'm gonna be a bad influence on him?" The bitterness that spills out is a surprise. I shouldn't still feel this way now Nate's told me it wasn't him who threw me under the bus. He just did a stupid thing and panicked, it was his dickhead stepdad and his lawyer who screwed me over. I just wish my own ma wouldn't have automatically assumed the worst of me.

She puts the knife down again and walks across the

kitchen to put her hands on my face. "I'm glad you two are close again."

Fuck, could I be any closer to blushing right now?

I squirm and she lets me go.

"You know Nate's welcome to stay over here?"

"We're not kids anymore, Ma. We don't have sleepovers."

The thought of having Nate in my bed again, this time knowing he wants to ... let's just say I don't trust myself with him in my bed.

"I'm just saying, he's welcome here any time."

I wanna tell her we can't just jump in a time machine and pretend the last five years never happened. That Nate didn't go off and have a totally different life. That he still lives next door and comes in and out of our house like it's his own. That Dad's gonna walk in through that door. My chest feels tight. Ma looks at me and frowns.

"You okay?"

"Indigestion," I lie.

"There's some Tums in the cupboard, take some."

"I'm fine, Ma, stop fussing."

My phone buzzes while I'm sitting at the table with my ma and Stacie. Ma's head shoots up straight away.

"Who is it?"

I try to keep the smile off my face when I answer. "Just Nate."

"Is he coming over?" Stacie asks, perking up.

I swear to god if he upsets her, I'm gonna kill him.

"No, he's got school stuff, I'm gonna meet him later."

"Aww, why don't you bring him here?"

"Yeah," Ma says. "Bring him to dinner."

I don't wanna bring him to dinner. I want him to fuck me again in the woods, before it gets weird, before he changes his mind and decides he's done experimenting. I'm on edge the way I was when I first started meeting strangers online. That new addiction, making you feel good, before it starts making you feel like shit. Making you ashamed of yourself for being so desperate. Like eating too much cake. It's good at first, and then suddenly you're stuffed and feel sick. Nate's still that first bite right now. The one that makes you ask why you don't eat cake for every meal.

The phone starts ringing, Nate's name flashing up on the screen. Stacie's hand shoots across the table and she grabs it before I can stop her. Those fucking hockey reflexes.

"Hi, Nate, it's Stacie."

I can hear Nate's voice through the phone and it makes the pit of my stomach tingle. Remembering his voice by my ear last night. Breathing hard while he pumped his cock in and out of my ass. Saying my name over and over as he came.

Stacie gets up from the table and starts telling him about hockey and school and some friend he's probably never met. He must keep asking her questions, because she's talking like it's a two-way conversation.

"Mom says you should come to dinner tonight."

My heart races as she waits for an answer. Her face lights up and she gives Ma a thumbs up.

"About seven okay?" she asks.

Fuck, she sounds so mature right now. My chest gets tight watching her. A couple of days ago, she couldn't stop crying over Dad. Now she's excited about something again, smiling, moving on. And it's because of Nate.

She puts the phone down and slides it across the table to me.

"You just hung up? How'd you know I didn't wanna talk to him?"

She shrugs. "He's coming over at seven, you can talk to

him then. He said he's got a mixer at the frat house though, so he can't stay."

I MEET the guys on the boardwalk. They're pissed off because I don't have any weed and when I call my guy, he's not picking up.

It's one of those days, walking around, looking for people, not finding anything. I'm actually relieved we don't find him. I don't wanna turn up stoned tonight for dinner with Nate and my family.

The guys go into a liquor store and come out with a bottle of vodka. When we go down to the beach to drink it, the tide's out and the sand seems to go on forever. I have to push out any thoughts of Nate, naked against the wall of showers, kissing him and making him come.

It's still light out, the sun red as it starts to set on the horizon. The guys don't even look at it, don't seem to notice as they pass the bottle around. I try to just take tiny sips when it's passed my way.

"What's wrong with you tonight, man?" Adam asks. He's in one of those moods, like he wants to terrorize someone. Usually the target's Paddy. He's small and kind of an idiot. But sometimes he's too much of an easy target. And when I don't have anything to offer, I'm just as disposable to him as Paddy is.

"I've got dinner with my ma and sister tonight."

They all laugh, like that's the cringiest thing they've ever heard.

"Oh, dinner with mommy, got it." Adam nods, staring at me as he takes his next swig. He shoves the vodka bottle against my chest and tells me to drink.

I take a swig and pass it to Paddy. He'll do whatever

Adam tells him to, but only if he gets what's going on. Right now, he looks buzzed and completely oblivious.

"Come on, let's go to the arcade."

We get out of there. I'm desperate to leave. I'll stay for another half hour then go home, drink some coffee and take a cold shower to sober myself up.

We're at the punchbag machine in the doorway of the arcade when this couple walks past, two guys. One of them is stroking the other guy's arm and they're looking into each other's eyes, smiling, happy, minding their own fucking business.

"Look at these two," Adam says, dropping a slur before spitting on the tarmac.

My stomach drops, my blood turns cold.

He makes a move towards them and I pull him back.

"What the fuck are you doing?" he snarls.

"Leave them be, man."

He frowns. "Why are you defending them?"

The couple walks past. I think Adam's stopped paying attention to them until he shouts the slur at them and makes to move. The couple stiffen but keep walking. Smart. I hope they keep going.

I push Adam against a claw machine, his back thudding against the Perspex, an alarm going off.

He shoves me back, so I shove him again. This time he grips me by the shirt and pulls me in.

Pain sears through my face before a trickle of warm fluid starts dripping from my nose. It takes me a beat to realize he's just headbutted me.

"Come on man, don't fight," Corey says, holding Adam back. Adam's grinning at me now, jutting his chin.

I shove him, pushing him and Corey back into the machine.

Employees from the arcade are coming over now, telling us they're calling the cops.

"Let's fucking go!" Corey starts running, dragging Adam with him, Paddy following close behind.

I'm dazed. *Which way should I go?* I sure as fuck don't wanna follow them, but I'm gonna get into trouble if I stay here.

One of the employees approaches me before I can make my mind up.

"Are you okay?"

"I'm fine," I wave him off.

"Are you sure? You're bleeding."

"I'm fine."

"Do you need anything?"

I think about going home to my ma and Stacie like this. I relax a little once I see he's not calling the cops—not right this second at least.

"Have you got some tissue or something?"

"Sure, come on in the back and clean up."

I give him a weary look.

"I'm not gonna call the cops on you, it obviously wasn't your fault."

I'm used to people automatically assuming it *was* my fault, but I don't have much choice but to get cleaned up before I show my face at home.

When I get back to the house, I've cleaned the blood off my face and I'm wearing a *Fun Times Arcade* t-shirt. My nose is swollen and sore but it's not broken. There's a bruise forming under one eye.

Nate's SUV is parked up at the end of the driveway. There's nothing I can do now. For some stupid reason, I think I might be able to pull it off. That they won't notice

I've just been headbutted and I'm wearing an arcade t-shirt that's two sizes too small.

I try to disappear upstairs to at least change my shirt, but Ma calls me out to the kitchen.

She gasps and her eyes go wide the second she sees me.

"Evan! Baby, what happened?"

I swat her hand away when she comes closer and tries to touch my face.

"Nothing Ma, I just got in a fight. It looks worse than it is."

"A fight? With who?"

"No one."

Nate and Stacie are standing at the table. They don't know where to look. I ruined dinner. My presence here has made everything worse.

"I'm gonna go and get changed."

Ma tries to call after me, but she trails off when she sees I'm not listening.

I lock the bathroom door and splash my face with water. I need ice. I need a fucking mask or something right now. There's no hiding the bruising or the swelling around my nose. *Fucking Adam.*

There's a knock on the door. I ignore it. They knock again.

"Who is it?"

"It's me." Nate. "Let me in."

He's not going away. I know how stubborn he is. With a sigh, I open the door. He comes in and locks it from the inside.

"What happened?" he asks, putting his hand on my face. I have to force myself not to close my eyes and surrender to it.

"I just got in a fight with a friend."

"A *friend* did this to you? Jesus, Ev."

I flinch from his touch and go back to the mirror.

"Are you okay?"

"I'm fine, I've had worse."

I pull the shirt off and leave it in a ball. I can feel Nate standing behind me, watching as I bend over the sink to wash my face. I know from experience it's possible to feel ashamed and turned on at the same time. That's how most of my hookups before Nate felt.

"Let me help."

I try to protest, but he presses me back against the sink and wets some toilet paper before dabbing up my nose.

"It's not broken."

"I know."

"Good." His lips twitch in a smile. "Because I'd be pissed if he messed up your pretty face."

He's talking quietly, but my heart still races at the thought of my ma or Stacie hearing him. I should tell him to shut up, but I don't want to.

"Oh yeah? What would you do?"

"I'd beat him up with my tennis racket."

I snort and he laughs.

"Shit," I say, remembering. "I didn't ask you how your game went. Who were you playing, Harvard, right?"

"It's called a *match,* and yeah, we won 7-0."

He tilts his face to kiss me and I catch his lips gratefully. They're—*he* is—like one fucking good thing in a sea of shit. I want to wrap myself up in his world. Tennis *matches* and country clubs. Even if it is fantasy. Even if it's only temporary.

"Does it hurt?" he asks. His voice is just above a whisper now.

"No, come here."

I pull him in by the waist, kiss him properly, my nose stinging when it squishes against his, but it's worth it.

I put my hands on his neck, kissing him deeply while I grind my cock against his and he sighs into my mouth.

"Evan," he pulls away, breathless, putting his hands on my chest to keep me at arm's length. "Fuck, I want to, but we can't. Not here."

"I know, relax. I was just teasing you."

"Asshole." He grins.

We're both smiling when we come back into the kitchen. Ma frowns at us.

"So, what's for dinner?"

I let Stacie steal Nate after dinner to play *NHL-something.* Nate doesn't even know the rules of hockey and I can hear her kicking his ass while I help Ma with the dishes.

She'd usually be smiling her head off over me helping her, about Nate being here, but she keeps side-eying me like she's gonna cry.

"Stop looking at me like that, Ma." I dry a plate and put it in the cupboard.

"I can't help it, you're my baby. I hate seeing you hurt."

"I'm not a baby, I'm twenty-years old."

"You'll always be my baby."

She hands me another plate after rinsing off the bubbles.

"I wish you'd stop hanging out with those losers."

I dry the plate and put it in the cupboard.

"Did one of them do this to you?"

"It was just a stupid fight, Ma. It happens."

"No, you and Nate never got into fights."

"Yeah, we did."

"You never came home like this."

"That's because Nate's a pussy."

She tuts at the word.

"Sorry, Ma."

Nate groans from the living room. I'm guessing Stacie scored on him again.

We wash and dry in silence. When Stacie starts singing "Another One Bites the Dust," I'm guessing she's struck the final blow on Nate's little hockey team.

I realize I don't want him to leave when we've finished washing the dishes and Stacie comes in to tell us she kicked Nate's ass. Even though it'd be hell lying next to him in bed, smelling his skin and staring at his lips, I want him here.

Nate's putting the controllers away when we come into the living room. It's weird how quickly we've started using this room again. I have to remind myself every time I walk in here that's it's alright.

"I'd better get going," Nate says.

"Why don't you stay over?" Ma asks.

"Um ... " he looks at me. "Sure, if it's okay."

"You can't," I say. Everyone turns and looks at me. "You've got that thing, at the frat house."

Nate shrugs. "It's not important, I don't have to go."

"Well then, that's settled." Ma says. "I'll get the air bed from the cupboard."

"I'll get it," I say.

Nate's face is bright red. He's rubbing the back of his neck. He's so bad at lying. He knows I'm not gonna make him sleep on a fucking air bed. But Ma would find it weird if we offered to sleep together.

We brush our teeth side-by-side in the little bathroom. Nate's using a spare toothbrush Ma found in the cupboard. I can hear Stacie talking on the phone in the next room while we settle into bed. Nate's wearing one of my old t-shirts and a revealing pair of boxer briefs that are gonna make it very fucking hard to fall asleep next to him.

His body heat radiates under the blanket. His skin brushing against mine every time he moves.

"Stay still."

"Sorry." His minty breath blows against my neck.

I can feel him trying to be still, but he's like a fucking puppy dog—all pent up energy with nowhere to go. I think about taking him out into the woods behind the house, letting him fuck me against a tree again, but I'm so tired. And weirdly, I want to lie here with him more. In the warmth and safety of my own bed.

"Ev?"

"What?"

He swallows. "Can I spoon you?"

I snort. "Seriously?"

"Yeah. It's okay if-"

I reach behind me and grab his arm, pulling it over my waist. "There. Happy?"

"Yeah."

I think he's gonna be quiet now, go to sleep. His body's pressed tight against me. His soft cock is warm against my back. If it was hard, I don't know if I'd be able to resist touching it.

"Ev?"

I blow out a big sigh. "What?"

"Are you happy?"

"What kind of question is that?"

"I know obviously you're not *happy*. I know you're going through a lot right now, but I mean, about this, *us*. You are happy about it, aren't you?"

Us? What's he talking about? Why does he have to do

this? Surely he understands why I don't expect him to hang around for this?

"Nate, it's been a long day, go to sleep."

I feel instantly guilty.

"Okay."

I know I won't be able to sleep until I say something back.

"I'm ... I'm glad you're here. Happy?"

I think I feel him smile against the back of my neck.

"Yeah. Me, too."

13

NATHAN

I'm tingling with nervous energy as I pull up to the house.

Waking up next to Evan in his bed again for the first time in years felt so right. Having breakfast with his family, laughing over his mom's pancakes. I felt like myself again, like I was exactly where I was supposed to be.

But there was a niggling doubt in the back of my mind, reminding me that Evan is still keeping me at arm's length. That he might still see me as just a hookup. And that maybe he's right to be worried.

A few of the guys give me sideways glances as I open the door.

"Hey man, you might want to make yourself scarce," Archer says.

"Why?"

"Nathan?" Priestley's voice is like a slap to the face. *Shit.*

"Is he really pissed about the-"

"Sorry dude," Archer slips into the living room as Priestley comes out of the executive office.

"Come with me."

I follow him, trying not to let my head drop. Squaring my shoulders as I enter the room.

"Close the door, Nathan."

I close it and head over to the chair in front of the big mahogany desk. Before I can take a seat, Priestley stops me.

"Did I say you can sit down?"

"Come on Priestley, this is ridiculous."

"Really? So you think it's okay to miss an important mixer without even calling to tell me you'd been in a terrible accident?"

I frown. "I wasn't in a terrible accident."

"Sorry, you must have been in the hospital then?"

I suck in a breath. I know what he's doing. "No."

"So you were getting laid?"

My face flushes. "I was not 'getting laid.'"

"No? But you *were* with this new guy."

I keep my mouth closed.

He sighs and rests his hands on the desk. "At least tell me you finished the financial reports for this quarter for the meeting tonight."

"Shit."

This time, there's no sigh. Just pure fury in his eyes as he pushes off the desk, nostrils flaring. "I'm not being the bad guy here, Nathan. This isn't fucking *Romeo and Juliet.* I already told you I don't give a shit about who you fuck, but when it starts getting in the way of your duties here, that's when I have to step in."

"What are you going to do?"

"This time, I'm going to give you a chance to get the report finished. Ask Harris for help, he's good at that stuff. But next time, you won't get another chance. I'll have no choice but to relieve you of your duties."

My stomach drops. I hadn't realized how important this

was until Priestley threatened to take it away. I imagine Bryce's reaction when he finds out I've been stripped of my VP duties. I'm about to thank him for giving me another chance when he interrupts me.

"Nathan, you know I'm only hard on you because I believe you have potential, right? I can't understand why you'd want to throw all of this away for some hookup."

"Evan is not a hookup."

He stares me down for a second. I hope he can see the challenge in my eyes. Eventually, he backs down, sighing.

"Whatever, you're dismissed."

I find Ben and spend the rest of the afternoon going over the financial reports for the quarter. Ben does most of the work. It usually takes me days to sort all these spreadsheets out and make sense of them, but Ben is a financial whiz and does it all in a couple of hours. When he's finished, we sit back and look at the results, feeling proud of ourselves. Well, Ben should feel proud of himself, I was a liability as usual.

"Thank you."

Ben blushes.

"And Ben, I'm sorry for being so caught up in my own shit that I've neglected you."

"It's okay."

An awkward silence follows and I'm desperate to fill it.

"By the way, Priestley told me to get you to help because you're good at this stuff."

"Priestley said I'm good at something?"

I laugh and he joins me. For a second, it's almost like nothing awkward has happened.

"I get the feeling he's hardest on the people he thinks have the most potential."

Ben rubs the back of his neck. "I don't know about that."

"You do know you're insanely smart and really good at all this stuff, right? That's exactly why I need you for our business. I couldn't do it without you."

He nods.

"And I'm also going to be the best wingman you've ever seen, this summer, it's going to be all about you getting laid."

His face flushes and he looks away. "I think I might be busy this summer."

I punch him lightly in the arm. "Whatever happens, Ben Harris will lose his virginity by the end of senior year."

I DRIVE STRAIGHT OVER to my mom and Bryce's house after the meeting at the frat, stopping the car out on the street so whatever car is taking my mom and Bryce to the airport can get in and out. Heaven forbid I hinder their escape. I want them gone just as much as they want to be gone.

Bryce is in the kitchen on the phone when I let myself in. He says goodbye and hangs up, smiling when he sees me with my weekend bag.

"Going to keep an eye on the place for us while we're gone, Nathan?"

Something bubbles in the pit of my stomach at the sound of his voice. He doesn't even notice. He's already tapping something into his phone.

"Bryce?"

"Yes?" he asks without looking up.

"Can I ask you something?"

"Sure, but be quick. The car's on its way. No wild parties by the way when we're gone." He looks up, grinning before he catches the look on my face. "Nathan, what's wrong?"

I take a deep breath, remind myself of how hurt Evan

was when he thought I'd thrown him under the bus. "Did you tell your lawyer to put the blame on Evan?"

He frowns. "What are you talking about?"

"Back when I crashed that car. Did you throw Evan under the bus to save my skin?"

He tuts. "Why are we talking about this now? It's all water under the bridge."

"You know it was my fault, right? You know *I* was drunk and stole that car. You know *I* was driving. Evan had nothing to do with it."

Bryce comes around the counter, his jaw set. "Your mother doesn't need this stress, just like she didn't need it back then. Regardless of whose fault it was, he was there when the police arrived, and if I used every means at my disposal to keep you out of trouble and stop you from getting a record, then sue me."

"It was juvenile, it wouldn't have mattered-"

He raises his voice. "Everything matters in our world. Don't you understand that? The stakes are much higher. The margin for error so much tinier."

"That's bullshit." I don't mean to say it, it just comes out. I see the shock on Bryce's face but can't stop myself.

"It's people like Evan who suffer when we screw them over. His stakes are whether or not he's going to be able to pay his bills this month. It's him who one mistake can fuck up forever. If he loses a paycheck, he's out on the street, you lose a paycheck? No fivestar luxury resort for you this year."

Bryce's face is red. He looks like he's going to blow his top before I see him visibly calm himself down, resting his hands on the waterfall counter and taking a deep breath. "Listen very carefully, Nathan. I took you on. I didn't need to. But if you're going to carry my name, you will behave accordingly and not embarrass me. I wasn't just protecting your reputation, I was protecting my own. I took a big chance marrying your mother and adopting you. But I love her, and so I did. You'd do well to remember how much I've given you."

He smooths his hand over his shirt and walks back around the counter, acting like I don't exist. My skin prickles and I go cold. Is this the man I've been trying to impress all these years? No matter what I do, will I always be a burden? Baggage he has to deal with if he wants my mom?

"Your mother wants to say goodbye to you before we leave, you should go up to her, and tell her to get a move on."

When I go upstairs, Mom's in the main bathroom, dressed in a cashmere sweater and putting cosmetics into a bag.

"There's plenty of food in the fridge, or I've left the number for Fiorentini's. They'll deliver if you tell them it's-"

"Ma, I'll just order Uber Eats."

She stiffens and I freeze.

"*Ma*?"

"Sorry. Slip of the tongue."

I take my weekend bag into my room and hope she doesn't follow, my heart hammering in my chest.

When I turn around, she's standing in the doorway, one skinny arm resting on the frame.

"What's going on with you?" she asks.

I shrug. "Nothing."

I start taking my clothes out of my bag and hope she'll be gone by the time I'm finished unpacking.

"Since when do you call me Ma?"

"Since I could talk," I shoot back.

I chance a look in her direction. She flares her nostrils, squaring her shoulders. The sight should be ridiculous. She must weight one-hundred pounds soaking wet. But she's my mother. The last thing I want to do is make her mad.

"Have you been with him?"

My face is burning when I ask, "Who?"

"You know who. Evan."

"Honey," Bryce calls from downstairs. "The car's here, we've got to go."

Mom stares at me from the doorway, waiting for an answer.

"Pamela?" Bryce shouts, more insistently this time.

She takes a deep breath and puffs her chest out. "We'll talk about this when we get back."

I grit my teeth and force myself to stay quiet as she leaves.

The second the door slams shut behind them, I sag with relief. But my mind is on overdrive as I wait for Evan to arrive. Telling me I'm fucking it all up. This opportunity. This life. I keep telling Evan it's not me. That it doesn't matter. But when was the last time I had nothing? Can I even remember what that was like?

EVAN HAS an early shift at the warehouse, so he's coming over straight after. I remind myself why he's worth the trouble. Think about him in his work pants and boots in that car. The smell of something unfamiliar on his clothes, like cardboard and dust. I want to take care of him. I want to run him a bath and get him a beer, but something tells me he wouldn't like that. He'd see straight through me, push away my attempts to try and make everything better.

Instead, I put a couple of pizzas in the oven and make sure there are chilled beers for us to drink if Evan wants one.

My mom or Bryce will probably notice they're gone, but they don't make a fuss about me drinking so long as I don't get sloppy or throw any wild parties. It's all about image, of course, I now realize. Do whatever you want, so long as you're quiet about it.

I don't like to think that's what I'm doing with Evan. But it's not like he's exactly open about what we're doing, either.

Evan's taking longer to get here than I thought he would. I'm pacing the living room, flipping through the channels for a movie or something to put on when the doorbell rings.

"Hey!" I can't keep the dopey grin from my face as I answer the door.

He isn't dressed in his work clothes. The thought of him going home to change before he came here makes my stomach flip.

He runs a hand over his shaved head and follows me into the house.

"Did you find the place okay? I would have picked you up from work-" I'm chattering on, I know, but I can't believe how nervous I am now he's actually here.

"It's fine," he interrupts.

"Want a beer?"

"Sure."

When I get to the kitchen, I take a deep breath, give myself a moment. Back in the living room, Evan's found the controller and is flipping through the channels. It's nice to see him semi-relaxed.

I hand him his beer and take a seat beside him on the sectional.

"Take your shoes off if you want. Make yourself comfortable."

"I'm good."

He lands on an episode of *Bob's Burgers* and I smile to myself.

"How was work?"

He shrugs. "Fine."

"I put some pizzas in the oven, they should be ready in a minute."

"Smells good."

We fall into an uncomfortable silence until my phone pings and I go to take the pizzas out.

I cut them up in the kitchen before bringing them back in.

Evan devours a few slices of pepperoni while watching the end credits to the cartoon.

"I'm surprised you're not watching football or some shit," he says, wiping his mouth on the paper towel I brought in.

"Why?"

He shrugs. "Just thought that's what jocks do."

I snort. "You do know tennis players are nerds, right?"

His eyebrow shoot up.

"Seriously. The football team, the hockey team, the lacrosse team ... fine. But the tennis team? A bunch of skinny nerds in polo shirts."

His eyes roam over my body and I feel my face flush.

"What about the frat thing?"

"Yeah, we're in the nerdiest fraternity on campus, too. The football players and a few of the hockey guys are in one of the neighboring frats—the party frat."

His lips quirk up on one side and he shakes his head. "I can't believe all that shit's actually real."

"What do you mean?"

"Like, it's not all just in movies. People are actually in ... " He does little air quotes "'Party frats.'"

My face gets even hotter and I rub the back of my neck. "Yeah, well...."

"What are the other guys like, in your 'not party frat?'"

"The guys are mostly okay. Ben—a guy I rushed with—he's a good guy, and he's on the tennis team, too. Things are a bit weird with Mark since he started dating my ex-girlfriend."

Evan's eyebrows shoot up again. "What happened to bros before hos?"

"Well, one—we don't call girls hos, and two—technically we'd broken up and he did ask my permission."

He shakes his head. "So, they're not hos, but you do have to call dibs?"

"No, not like-"

"What's your role in this nerdy fraternity, then?"

It's the first time he's called it something other than a 'frat' with an air of disdain. I'm still embarrassed to tell him what my role is, but it would be weird if I ignored the question.

"I'm Vice President."

Now he smiles. It's not a totally mocking smile.

"That's actually impressive."

"I thought you'd think it's stupid."

"I do. But if you're gonna be a part of something stupid, might as well be the vice president of it."

I punch him in the arm and he laughs.

Another episode of *Bob's Burgers* starts playing and I settle in to watch it, just enjoying having Evan here by my side. But something uneasy won't settle inside me.

"I confronted Bryce today."

He freezes with his hand over the pizza box. "Nate, I don't want you to-"

"I needed answers."

He brings his hand back into his body. "What did he say?"

"He was just looking after his interests. He didn't really care who was in the wrong so long as his reputation wasn't damaged."

"Sounds about right."

"Evan, am I really stupid?"

He frowns. "No."

"I feel like I've been the most oblivious person on the planet these past few years and now I'm just opening my eyes."

"What do you mean?"

I think about Ben. About Bryce. I can't tell him about Ben, that's his private business.

"Just everything with you and Bryce and my mom. I feel like I've been walking around in a bubble, not seeing things how they really are."

He looks up at me through his fair lashes and I can't stop myself from stroking his face. He closes his eyes and presses against my palm and I feel it all shuck away. All the stress and uncertainty. Evan was always the one person I could rely on. How could I fuck it up so badly?

He eats more of the pizza, takes his shoes off, and puts his feet up on the coffee table full of coffee table books about architecture and modern art.

I watch him from the corner of my eye. Admiring the way he looks in his sweatpants and white t-shirt. The shape of his feet in socks. I haven't really gotten to admire him when we've been together before, on the dark beach or squashed up in my car. I imagine him on my bed, hovering over me. The St. Christopher he's worn since we were kids dangling over my face.

When the next episode finishes, I ask him if he wants a tour of the house.

I'm embarrassed by most of it and try to make fun of everything. Like Mom's waterfall island counter and Bryce's stupid fish tank.

"What's down there?" Evan asks when I pass the door to the basement.

"A pool."

"Seriously?"

I rub my neck. "Stupid, right?"

"Show me."

I open the door and lead him down the stairs. They're not rickety like the kind we had in my old house. I was always scared of that basement. The boiler that made a weird, moaning noise. The rats you'd hear scurrying as soon as you turned the light on.

This basement is bright and white and free of rats and moaning boilers. Just the hum of the pool cleaner or filter or whatever keeps the pool warm and clean.

Lights under the surface bathe the pool in a greenish hue. Evan blinks at everything like he's just stepped into Wonderland.

"Do you actually swim down here?"

"Sometimes," I shrug. "Bryce uses it every morning."

When I turn around, Evan's stripping down to his boxers. "You comin'?"

I follow him, watching him jump in, splashing water over the mosaic tiles.

The water's warm, as always. Evan floats in the middle of the pool, his legs a wobbly blur underneath him.

He ducks his head under before coming up again, water dripping from his nose and eyelashes.

"This is cool."

"You don't think it's ostentatious and douchey?"

"Oh, totally."

Something twists in my stomach.

"Hey, what's up?"

"Nothing, I just don't want you to think I'm a rich asshole. All of this ... " I throw my gaze up to the ceiling, the spotlights shining down on us. "It's not mine. It's Bryce's."

Evan's treading water, his legs kicking under him.

"Listen, I get it. You're not your stepdad."

I smile and nod, but I don't fully believe him.

He grabs my hand under the water. When I drag my gaze up, he's looking right at me.

He swims a little closer and presses his lips against mine. I wrap my legs around his waist, feeling him hard against me. The kiss intensifies until he's pushing me back against the edge of the pool.

I let my arms drape over his shoulders and give into him. Letting him take the lead, as always. His fingers slip inside the waistband of my boxer briefs and tug, the water causing some resistance. I help him by wriggling free, kicking them off when they bunch around my ankles.

He slides his hands under my thighs and pushes me up, until I'm out of the water and sitting on the edge of the pool. Before I can say anything, Evan has my cock in his mouth and is blowing me with that same expert skill I remember from last time. I put my hand on the back of his shaved head and watch it bob between my legs.

My stomach tingles and my toes curl under the water.

"Fuck, Evan, like that."

I rest back on one hand, keeping the other on Evan's head, tilting my own so I can watch him. His cheeks hollow as he takes me into his throat and swallows.

I throw my head back and let out something between a

moan and a whine. I don't fucking know what. I just know that whatever Evan's doing to me right now feels so good, I can't think straight. I want to tell him to stop. I want to do what we did that night. Replicate how close I felt to him. His smell in my nostrils. His salty skin pressed against my lips. Making him feel good, listening to him moan and say my name.

But his lips feel too good wrapped around my dick. His tongue dragging along the underside, pressing against that throbbing vein. Licking around the head of my leaking cock.

I give into it. Throw my head back and close my eyes. Moan like a porn star while Evan sucks my cock, giving me the best blow job of my life.

I come, shuddering and cursing like a sailor. Evan doesn't stop until I'm milked dry. He turns and spits into the pool, wiping his mouth with the back of his arm.

"Now your dickhead stepdad has your cum in his pool."

"Holy shit."

He laughs.

"You're crazy."

He swims backward. I want to join him, but I'm boneless. I don't even know if I could stand right now. Getting back in the pool is the worst idea.

I manage to push myself up enough to stand. "Let's go to my room."

Evan's erection is visible under the water, and I want to take care of that. Take care of him the way he took care of me.

I wring my underwear out in the pool, Evan's suggestion I leave it there for Bryce to find a step too far. He grins at me like he wants to call me a choir boy or something equally angelic, but he refrains.

I don't bother telling him the pool will clean itself by the time Bryce comes back from the Bahamas. Just the thought of getting one over on him after what I've learned recently is enough to warm me a little.

My underwear's too wet to put back on, so I climb the stairs completely naked. Evan's behind me, and the thought of him watching my ass makes my skin prickle and my cock twitch.

"This is my room," I say, stepping into the nondescript bedroom. Cream walls, a double bed with crisp, white bedsheets under the window with cream-colored curtains. Matching nightstands I filled with condoms and lube in anticipation of Evan's visit. Some textbooks on the desk. A few novels and old comic books on the bookshelf.

"Where's all your dorky posters?" Evan asks.

"What dorky posters?"

"Those ones you used to have when we were kids?"

"I'm a little old for Pokémon, don't you think?"

He laughs, crossing the room until he's standing right in front of me.

"So what's the grown up version of dorky posters? The periodic table? Einstein quotes?"

"That's all at my room at the frat house."

"Ah, yeah, shit, I forgot about that for a second."

My face heats up.

"You think it's lame."

"What?"

"Me being in a frat—me being a 'frat boy'?"

His lips quirk up. "I dunno, I guess it could be kinda hot."

My heart sinks. I don't want it to be hot. I want Evan to like me. To see *me*.

"What's up?" he asks.

"Nothing."

He tilts my face up gently to look at him. "I'm sorry, okay? I was being a dick."

I shake my head. "It doesn't matter."

I take his hand before kissing him, then dropping to my knees. I catch the slightest gasp from Evan and it gives me so much satisfaction to know he wants this.

Hooking my thumbs into the waistband, I tug his underwear down, inch by agonizing inch. When I glance at Evan, he's watching me. His lips slightly parted, eyes hooded.

His cock springs free and before I can overthink it, I lick the underside of the tip. Relishing his taste. Lapping up the pre-cum beading on his head. He groans, burying his hand in my hair. I take these little encouragements to heart and wrap my lips around his head, before burying his cock as far back as it will go.

Evan sucks in a breath through his teeth. "*Fuck,* Nate, that's good."

I moan around him and he groans again.

I'm getting hard. I didn't realize how much I'd like this. How fucking *good* it would feel sucking Evan's cock. His weight and taste and the musky smell of his skin so close.

"Fuck, that's it." He runs his hand through my hair, grasping at the back.

I moan around him while I stroke myself, feeling so out of control I'm dizzy.

When Evan pulls his dick out of my mouth, I look up at him, feeling drunk.

"Get on the bed," he says, his voice raspy.

I do as I'm told, surprised when my legs actually move how I want them to.

Evan moves toward me and I take in every inch of his body. The definition of his abs and the veins in his biceps and forearms. The St. Christopher sitting between his collarbones and the freckles dotted over his shoulders.

My heart catches, feeling like it jumped into my throat. The boy I've loved my whole life is standing right in front of me, except, he's a man now. And he wants me.

Evan guides me back onto the mattress and lies down beside me, top and tail like how we used to sleep when I'd stay over at his house. He starts planting little kisses on my thighs before brushing his lips along my cock. It's still a little sensitive, but I let him do it. His brushes turning to licks until he's wrapping his lips around it and sucking.

His cock is rock hard between us. I guide him by the hips until I can comfortably wrap my lips around him and suck him back as far as I can take it.

"That okay, Nate?" he asks, pulling out. I look down and nod. "Sure?"

"Yes."

He guides his cock back between into my lips, rubbing the head across my mouth first in a way that makes my cock jump.

"That's it," he says and I moan around him again. "*Fuck*, Nate, that's it."

His praise makes my head swim. I love it. I want more. I move my head with his thrusts, forcing him back into my throat, resisting the urge to gag. His breath hitches and his hand tightens on my ass as he guides my cock back between his lips.

Saliva pools and drips down the sides of my mouth, but I don't care. Evan's cock is dripping with my spit and the precum I manage to lick up and smear down his shaft before he thrusts deeper each time.

I whimper around him and he pulls out.

"Okay?"

I nod. My eyes are watering, tears dripping down my face.

He sits up and kneels in front of me. "Sure?"

He grabs my face in his hands and kisses me spit, precum, and all.

"Yeah." I manage to get a hold of myself and wipe my face with the back of my arm. "Put your cock back in my mouth, I wanna make you come."

He groans, planting kisses on my neck and cheeks.

"I'd rather come while you fuck me, like last time."

"Really?"

"Yeah. Did you like it?"

I nod.

I gasp at Evan's hand on my cock, his thumb teasing over the head. "I've got condoms, but they're in my pants downstairs," he says

"Don't worry, I've got condoms and lube in the drawer."

"Good."

He moves to the top of the bed on his knees, facing the headboard.

I slide in behind him, but this isn't how I want to fuck him, not this time.

I kiss the back of his neck, tracing the shape of the freckles lining the backs of his shoulders.

"I love these," I say, my voice hoarse.

"What?"

"Freckles."

He snorts. "I hate 'em."

"Why? They're so hot."

He hums like he disagrees but he won't bother arguing. I take my time tracing his hips with my fingers, ghosting my hands over his shoulder blades, his spine, those dents in his lower back, pressing my thumbs into them, seeing how well they fit.

Evan groans. "Fuck, Nate, do it already."

"Patience. Let me enjoy you. I've waited a long time for this."

He goes completely still and I keep running my hands over his beautiful skin. Noting the tan lines where his shorts usually sit. He must walk around without a shirt on when he's on the beach, because he doesn't have any tan lines where a shirt or vest would be. I stroke his pale ass cheeks, watch him shiver as I get closer to his crack. He opens his legs wider and grips the headboard. Pressing my lips to his shoulder, I sigh, closing my eyes before nipping his skin, letting my tongue trace a cluster of freckles, tasting the saltiness of his sweat and chlorine from the pool.

"I want you," I whisper. "So bad."

"Fuck, Nate, you're gonna kill me with this shit."

I don't even think about what he might mean by that. Instead, I open the drawer and take out the box of condoms and the new tube of lube and throw them on the bed. Evan looks at them as I stroke the inside of his thigh. His cock is leaking, pre-cum dripping down his shaft.

When my fingertips finally graze his balls, he gasps. I start massaging them and he grinds his ass back against my cock. I know he can feel it. How turned on I am for him. I want him to know how much I want him. Need him.

We grind as I slide my hand up and down his length. Silent. Our breath and the friction of skin are the only sounds in the room. I don't even need to be inside him, I could come just like this. But he's pushing back with more insistence, so I pop the cap on the lube and slide my fingers into his crack and he hisses. My finger finds his hole and I rub circles around him until he lets me in with a groan.

I clamp my mouth down on his shoulder and suck as I massage him with my fingertips, hooking my fingers until his legs start to shake.

With two fingers buried deep inside him, he says, "Now, *fuck.* Nate, do it."

"You open the condom, please."

He tears into the box and rips the condom packet open with his teeth before passing it back to me.

I wish I could just sink into him with my bare skin, but I wouldn't do that. Even if I'm half mad in the moment and would do anything Evan asked, I want to protect him.

I slick myself up with the lube before pressing against his hole. Evan groans and lets his head fall forward, but I pause.

"What the fuck, Nate? Just do it."

"Turn around."

"What?"

"Please, Ev. I need to see your face while I do this."

He turns, his pupils blown wide and a flush crawling from his chest up his neck and face.

Fuck, I'm so glad I made him turn around.

I ignore the faded bruise under his eye, grabbing his face and kissing him hard, savoring the shape of his lips and the way he tastes.

He pulls away, scooting down onto his back and wrapping his legs around me.

"Like this?"

"Yeah."

"Come on, then."

His St. Christopher sticks to his chest with sweat as I spread his legs and watch his lids droop. He bites his lip when I start to sink into him. I sink half way in and stroke his cock as I go deeper. His eyelids flutter and he moans when I bottom out.

"Fuck you, Nate."

I catch his lips on a smile before starting to move.

I look down at him while I thrust, slow and deep.

"I never thought it'd be like this," I say.

"Like what?"

"I thought you'd have me bent over a desk or something."

His gaze shoots to the desk in the corner of the room. "If that's what you want, we'll do that later."

I thrust a little harder and his breath hitches.

"I want you in every way imaginable. I want you in every part of this room." I thrust on every breath. "In every position."

"Fuck, Nate."

His cock slaps against his stomach as I speed up my thrusts, fucking him into the mattress, gauging from his face what he wants. Every time I speed up or thrust harder, he encourages me with a "yes" or a "like that" and "that's it."

I feel my orgasm start to build and wrap my hand around his cock.

"No, I'm too close," he says.

"Me, too. Come with me."

He keeps his eyes on me, hands gripping the pillow behind his head. The veins in his biceps are bulging and the soft blond hairs in his armpits glisten with sweat.

His cock throbs in my hand and his body grows rigid, his head shooting off the bed. His eyes roll back on a deep moan and his ass starts to clench and pulse around my cock. I let my body lead as I milk every last drop from him until he bats my hand away.

He's watching me as I spill the last trickles into the condom, his arms still above his head.

I pull out, gently dropping his legs back onto the bed before lying down beside him.

We're silent for a while, but it's not the uncomfortable silence of an hour ago. It's content. Awed—at least on my side.

Eventually, Evan sits up. "I'm gonna clean up." He disappears into the bathroom and comes back with a damp towel to clean his cum off me. I want to tell him not to bother. I plan on getting him dirtier, much dirtier. Over and over and over again.

14

EVAN

Nate's fucking insatiable. He barely let me sleep last night and I woke up this morning to his hand stroking my belly. The second he realized I was awake, that hand slid lower while he seemed to be doing his best to give me a hickey on the back of my neck. When I asked him what he was doing, he just snickered and said, "You can tell people it's a bruise."

Yeah okay, not everyone lives in Naïve-Land. I wanted to say. But then I remembered him asking me if he was stupid, and stopped myself.

After he finally lets me out of bed and into the shower—with him, obviously—we eat a good portion of the fancy food in his fridge and Nate makes coffee in some weirdly complicated coffee machine with Italian words all over it. He keeps grinning at me and it's weirdly contagious. For a second, I can forget the fact I'm in Nate's parents' mansion and that I definitely don't belong here. If they knew, they'd probably have me arrested or set the dogs on me or something.

When I look up, Nate's frowning at me. "What's up?"

I rub the back of my neck, embarrassed he clocked me so fast. "Does your stepdad have dogs?"

"No, why?"

"No reason."

He hums to himself while he operates the coffee machine in his grey sweats. The fabric hugs his nicely toned ass. He was bullshitting me when he said tennis players were skinny nerds. Nate, at least, has the body of those hockey players Stacie's always watching on YouTube. "What are you doing today?"

"I've got a shift later."

His head pops up from the machine, a big smile on his face. "So you're free?"

Shit. No, I should go and see my guy, get more weed to sell. Bill day is coming up fast. I hesitate, trying to come up with a good excuse.

He's giving me those puppy dog eyes.

"My next match in the Ivy's coming up," he says like he knows I'm trying to find a way to say no. "I thought maybe you could help me train."

"Why me? Don't you have teammates for that?"

He shrugs. "I'm not really on good terms with my frat president right now, and he's also captain of the tennis team."

"What happened?"

He shrugs. "Nothing. He can just be a lot sometimes." He forces a smile and pulls me in by the waistband of my pants. "And anyway, I'd rather spend time with you. I thought we could go for a run on the beach."

"I don't run."

He snorts. "So how are you so in shape?" His eyes roam over my body and I almost fucking blush.

"I lift weights. I don't run."

"You're lucky, you must have a good metabolism. I start to get a muffin top if I eat too much pizza and don't do enough cardio."

My heart sinks. I pull him in tighter and grip his hips. "So fucking what? Get a muffin top."

He laughs, burying his face against my neck. Fucking hell. That fresh sweat smell drives me crazy.

"I'll watch you run on the beach, if that helps?"

His head snaps up. "Really?"

"Yeah, really. But only for an hour or so. There's some shit I have to do today."

He frowns. "You're not going to see those guys who gave you a black eye, are you?" His gaze strays to the fading bruise under my right eye. The bridge of my nose still hurts a bit, but it's nothing I can't handle.

"No. It's something else. And I haven't got a black eye."

He raises one eyebrow. "Like what?"

I loosen my grip on him and step back. "Nothing."

"Is it another guy?"

"What? Fuck. No, obviously not."

He looks sad now. *Fuck.*

I take a deep breath. "Listen, it's not a big deal. But to make a bit of extra cash, I've been moving some stuff for a guy I know."

I wait for his reaction, trying not to let it show on my face that I'm scared he'll be disappointed.

He frowns, obviously turning it over in his head.

"What do you mean, 'moving stuff'? Evan, are you selling drugs?"

I roll my eyes and try to act like it's not a big deal. "It's just weed. I won't do pills or anything like that. Weed's not even illegal here anymore."

"So why do people need to buy it off you? You don't have

a license to sell it, right? And you'd get in trouble if you were caught?"

"Do you know how expensive dispensary weed is? You don't have to pay taxes to a dealer. Anyway, I'm careful. I told you, it's not a big deal."

"Do you need money?"

"Obviously. Who doesn't? And before you offer, no you can't loan or give me any." *No way, I'm not letting Nate give me money.* The memory of that night resurfaces—two greasy fifty-dollar bills on a stranger's dashboard. It won't be like that with Nate. It can't be.

"Evan."

"It's fine, okay? Just stop stressing."

He bites his lip. I swear if he carries on, I'm gonna have to take him back to bed or something to shut him up, and I don't know if my dick, or my ass, can take anymore.

"Okay?" I put my hand on his arm.

He looks up finally, nodding. "Please be careful, Ev."

My heart does a stupid flutter. I know my ma and Stacie care about me, but I haven't had anyone verbalize it like this for a long time.

"I will be. Don't worry."

Nate drives us to the beach in his SUV and I watch him run laps in the sand, timing him on my phone for some reason. It doesn't matter how fast he does it, he isn't an Olympic sprinter, but I humor him. Because it seems to make him happy.

"What was my time this time?"

"Slower."

"Damnit."

I snort. "Go again."

Families explore the beach as Nate gets ready to run another lap. Kids are wading into the sea. People are washing their dogs at the showers. I try not to think about Nate pressed against the wall. His eyelids fluttering as he spilled over my knuckles.

"Evan?"

"Yeah?"

"What was my time?"

"Oh, shit. Sorry, I forgot to press start. Go again."

I realize he'll keep running until I tell him to stop, so I let him off the hook and buy him a water ice cone and watch him eat it. His sweat has made a dirty band around his cap.

"I'm gonna rinse off in the shower. Come with?" He waggles his eyebrows and bursts out laughing. "You should see your face."

I LET Nate play whatever the fuck emo music he wants in the car before he drops me off at work. It's a bad idea to let him drive me here. I shouldn't let him anywhere near my work, but it's too late now. He's already wormed his way back in with Ma and Stacie. Might as well infiltrate my place of work, too.

I try not to watch his left knee bouncing in his sweats while he drives. Try not to catch his smell being circulated around the car with the air conditioning. Definitely try not to think about him fucking me in every part of his room. *Fuck,* I haven't come that many times in one day since I was like sixteen.

He keeps glancing over at me and grinning. Maybe I should be self-conscious or ashamed or whatever—letting Nate see me like that, bent over his desk and hungry for his cock. Practically begging him to give it to me. But all I'm thinking is that I can't wait to do it again.

I'm only semi-sane again once I've climbed out of the car. "I'll pick you up at eleven," he says as I get out.

I watch as he drives away, trying to will myself back into the real world.

Bob catches me coming in.

"Hey Evan, how's it going?"

I realize I'm grinning like an idiot and wipe the smile off my face.

"Okay, thanks."

His face changes once he looks at me properly.

"What happened to your face? Everything okay?"

"I just hit it with the door. Don't worry about it."

He looks like he isn't gonna drop it. I consider making a joke about Ma hitting me with the frying pan, but I don't think he'd find it funny. Thankfully he nods and accepts my explanation. As he's walking away, something comes over me.

"Hey, Bob. Do you think I could get the application form for that course?" My neck starts to heat up, but I force myself to hold his gaze and ignore the stupid grin that spreads over his face. He practically trips over himself getting it for me.

After I clock in, I take up my space at the packing machine and get to work.

I have to force myself to keep my phone in my pocket. I told Nate I can't text him or anything while I'm at work, but I still wanna see if he texted anyway.

Images of us in his room, or in the pool, keep floating to the surface, making me smile. My face gets hot and my pants are suddenly too tight.

I never thought I'd get to hear the way Nate sounds

when he moans. Or see his face when he comes. Never thought I'd be the one to make that happen. Now it has, it feels surreal. It's fucking scary. What am I gonna do if Nate decides this isn't for him? No, not *if*. When.

I don't even look at my phone while I take my break in the back. I grab a Snickers from the vending machine and a scorching cup of watery coffee and ignore the clock on the wall.

When I told my ma I was crashing at Nate's, she had this big smile on her face. I wanted to tell her that me and Nate are fucking, just to see her reaction. Would she still love him then? Would she still think he was a good influence?

I know my ma isn't homophobic. She fucking hates that shit. She loves everyone. Thinks everyone should be treated with the same kindness. But would she feel differently if she knew her son was gay? Would she, at the very least, be worried? I don't want to be another reason she worries. I never want her to have to worry about another thing in her life. Thinking about my ma's possible reaction to me coming out, I start to wonder what Dad might have thought. I saw him defend a guy from some homophobic hate crime once. I didn't understand what was happening at the time, and I don't know whether he just thought it was unfair that there were three or four guys against one, or if he really thought it was wrong to be a homophobic prick. I'll never get to ask him now. What I do know, beyond any shadow of a doubt, is that he loved Nate. Loved him like a son. Would he think it was weird us fucking? Did he want me to see Nate as a brother and nothing more? Or would he be relieved that I was doing this with someone he approved of with all his heart?

Clocking off time rolls around and I can't fucking wait to

see Nate sitting out there in his stupid SUV, waiting for me with a smile on his face.

I exit quickly, before all the women come out of the locker room in their big groups, huddling outside to smoke their cigarettes before they go home to their husbands and kids. Nate's car is already in the lot. The headlights come on when he starts the engine.

I'm heading towards it when I hear someone call my name. The familiar voice makes my insides turn to ice. I glance over my shoulder to see Paddy jogging over to me. Behind him, Adam and Corey are leaning against the parking lot barrier.

"Hey man, what's up?" Paddy asks.

"Adam send you to do his dirty work?" I try to walk past him, but Paddy blocks my way. I know I could easily put him on his ass, but I don't want to shoot the messenger. I know he's just doing what Adam told him to do. Trying to fit in.

"He's sorry-"

Adam starts walking over, tossing his smoke away as he reaches me. I try not to let my gaze flicker to Nate, praying he'll stay in the fucking car.

"Hey man, let's forget about that stupid fight, yeah?"

I shrug and stick my hands in my pockets, hoping he won't push. "It's a little soon to forget for me. Let's talk tomorrow, okay?"

But Adam doesn't back off like I'm hoping. "Don't be like that."

My stomach drops at the sound of a car door slamming shut.

"Everything okay?" Nate's voice. *Fuck.*

"It's forgotten, okay?" I tell Adam, hoping to fuck he'll keep his attention on me and not turn it on Nate.

"Who the fuck are you?" Adam asks Nate. No such luck.

Everything in me stiffens, ready for a fight. If he even so much as fucking looks at Nate wrong, I don't think I'll be able to control myself.

"Nate, get back in the car, I'll be there in a second."

Even though I don't take my eyes off Adam, I can tell Nate is hovering between us and the car. Why can't he listen to me without needing to know why, just this once?

"Is that little Nate Castellani?" Adam asks, a hint of a snarl in his tone. "He your boyfriend now, Evan?"

Paddy pulls on his arm. He's like the kid in a divorce, hating his mom and dad fighting, trying to keep the peace. Even if it means getting caught in the crossfire.

I shake my head. "Come on, Nate."

As I turn, Adam pulls me back by my sleeve.

"I'm talking to you," he says.

Adrenaline pumps through my blood, circulating my odds. There's three of them—two and a half, really—and one of me. I meant what I said to Ma about Nate being a pussy. And I fucking like that he's not a fighter. I don't want him to ever have to fight a day in his life, especially not because of me.

If I just walk away, Adam's gonna think I'm soft. Soft people get walked all over. Guys like Adam, they get a kick out of it. I already let him headbutt me, doesn't matter that the fight got stopped before I could retaliate. He's not gonna see it like that.

I push him as hard as I can, nearly knocking him on his ass. I can hear Nate saying my name behind me, but I have to block it out. I can't be the guy who goes all fucking gooey at the sound of Nate's voice, not right now.

Before Adam can retaliate, I throw a right hook. It catches him on the jaw and his head snaps back. My stomach roils at the crack of my fist making contact. I don't like violence either, but sometimes it's necessary.

Paddy just stands there, waiting for someone to tell him what to do. But Corey's running over now, his footsteps getting faster the closer he gets. He shoves me and I shove back. Adam recovers from the hit to the jaw and comes at me, asking Paddy why he's just standing there.

They all come at me.

Nate steps in the way.

"Look at this pretty boy," Adam says, leering at Nate. He knocks the cap off his head and I fucking lose it.

"Get your fucking hands off him."

"Fuck me, he *is* your boyfriend, isn't he? I knew you were a fucking fa-"

I throw another punch and he grabs my jacket and holds on. I feel someone punching me in the back of the head. See their faces up close, snarling, like a pack of dogs. Everything is fists and grunts and the sound of flesh getting smacked. I don't know where Nate is. I just know I have to fight my way out to protect him. I hope to fuck he ran back to his car or to the warehouse to get help.

I don't notice people coming out of the back of the warehouse until Bob's voice is raised above them all.

Big, meaty hands are between us, prizing us apart, and then the guys are running for the trees, shouting shit over their shoulders and Bob's gripping me tight by the arms to hold me back.

Some of the women gather around, asking if I'm alright.

"I'm fine." I shake Bob off.

I look around for Nate. He's on the ground. My stomach drops.

"Nate!"

He looks up, grabbing his arm. There's a little bit of blood under his nose, dirt on his face, but apart from that, he looks okay. I check him over anyway. Not giving a shit who's watching.

"You okay? You hurt?"

He shakes his head, but he's wincing and still grabbing his arm.

"Who the hell was that?" Bob asks. It's the first time I've ever heard him raise his voice. My stomach drops again. *Fuck, could I lose my job?* Someone is saying they've called the police. My head spins. I pull Nate to his feet, trying to usher him toward the car.

"Oh no, you don't," Bob says. "Come inside, let me get you cleaned up."

"We're fine. I'm sorry, I can't get in trouble with the cops."

"You won't get in trouble," Bob says.

One of the women pipes up. "We all saw, those guys jumped you, you didn't do anything wrong. You were defending yourself. It was three on one."

"I called an ambulance, too," one of them says.

"We're fine."

"No, you're not," Bob says. "You're hurt, and so is he."

Nate's really wincing now, holding his arm to his chest like a broken wing. *Fuck, no.*

"Come on." Nate's voice snaps me out of my fury.

"Let's go inside like your boss says."

I nod, picking Nate's cap up off the ground as I follow them inside.

Bob's office has a first aid kit. I sit in one of the plastic chairs in front of his desk while he opens it and takes out some antiseptic and cotton balls.

"Are you gonna tell me what happened out there?" Bob asks.

He looks from me to Nate, but we both keep our mouths shut.

"I guess not." He dabs some antiseptic on a cotton ball before holding it to my eyebrow. "This might sting."

I flinch and hiss when he dabs the cotton against the cut.

"Sorry."

"You're not gonna say anything to my ma, are you?"

Bob takes a deep breath. "I think it's a bit too serious for that, Evan. Plus, your mother has a right to know if you're hurt."

"She's got enough to worry about."

He nods. "I know that. But we'll let her decide."

He dabs some more antiseptic in my cut and I manage to hold back a hiss this time.

"Who were those guys?"

"Just some friends."

Bob scoffs. "Some friends."

"And this guy?" Bob gestures to Nate, sitting in the other chair, looking at us with big eyes while Bob cleans my cut out.

"That's Nate. An old friend."

"Guess old friends are better than new ones, huh?"

"Yeah, I guess."

Nate's sitting in the chair, nursing his arm. Under the harsh lighting in Bob's office, I can see that something's seriously wrong with his wrist. It's like the bone is more pronounced, like it's poking out at a weird angle. He offers me a weak smile before dropping his eyes.

Once Bob is done fussing at me, I go to finish cleaning myself up in the bathroom. The dingy mirror shows that the cut across my eyebrow and some bruising on my jaw are the worst of it. The back of my head is killing, but as I gingerly explore the area with my fingertips, there aren't any cuts there. For a few extra seconds, I just stand at the sink, dreading going back out there.

I can't believe I got him hurt.

An ambulance and a police car show up. The police ask me questions while the EMTs look us over. Nate's immediately taken into the ambulance and I'm separated from him while the cops ask me the same questions over and over.

"Who were the guys who jumped you?"

"I don't know," I lie. "Just some guys."

Bob gives me a side-eye.

"Just some guys knew where you worked and jumped you for no reason?" the cop asks.

I hear one of the women who stuck around to give evidence tell a female cop that it sounded like a homophobic hate crime. My face flushes. Is everyone in work going to know I'm gay now? Will someone tell my ma? Nate's in an ambulance, maybe with a broken wrist because of me, now my ma might find out from some woman at the grocery store that her son's gay, the same way I found out about Dad's cancer spreading, because I was too chicken shit to tell her myself.

The cops sigh and close their notepads. "If you don't give us any information, we can't do anything to help you."

"I'm sorry." I shrug. "I don't know what else to tell you. I don't know the guys, they just jumped us, I've never seen them before."

When they put me in the ambulance with Nate, I can't even look at him. I've never felt more ashamed in my life.

15

NATHAN

I push down my panic over the searing pain in my wrist. The last time I dared take a peek at it, the bone looked all weird and was definitely not where it was supposed to be. I don't think it's going to be any different when I look at it again.

Evan is sitting in the ambulance on the bench opposite mine, his head down. His eye and lip are already starting to swell.

We play Cornell tomorrow. We're in the middle of the Ivy and weeks from regionals and I've probably broken my wrist. Even if it's not broken, it's definitely sprained—and I won't be holding a racket by my first match. My eyes fill and I sniffle and wipe my face with the back of my hand.

We're separated at the hospital while I go to get some scans. The painkillers the EMT gave me are starting to kick in. The pain is subsiding a little and I feel woozy. But that panic is gnawing at the back of my head. Clawing to get out.

"Where's Evan?"

"Your friend's just getting some tests. He took a few

knocks to the head. We want to make sure there's no concussion."

"I don't know if he has insurance." I don't think I was supposed to say that, but the meds are making my tongue loose. The nurse props my pillow up, her expression never changing from neutral. "Don't you worry yourself about it, we'll figure all that out later. You just relax and wait for the doctor."

I'm taken in for a scan before being chaperoned back to my bed. When my phone is returned to me, I have a ton of missed calls and messages from my mom.

Fuck.

I hit call, still feeling a little out of my head.

"Nathan, Jesus, why didn't you answer your phone? We're on our way back."

"On your way back from where?"

"The Bahamas!"

"Why?"

"Why do you think?"

I frown. "I don't know."

"Nathan, you were in an accident. The hospital called."

"Why would they call? I'm fine. Seriously. I just hurt my wrist, it's not a big deal. I had worse injuries doing stupid stuff when I was a kid."

She sounds teary when she speaks again. "I told you to stay away from him. I knew you'd get hurt if you got involved with him again."

"Mom, this wasn't Evan's fault."

"So he was there?"

"These guys just jumped him, he didn't even do anything wrong."

"I can't believe it." It sounds like she's muttering to

herself now. I'm so tired, I could fall asleep sitting up. I let the phone drop onto the bed and close my eyes.

"Nathan! Nathan? Are you still there?"

"Hm? Mom, I'm tired, can I call you back later?"

"Baby, don't fall asleep, you might have a concussion."

I laugh, feeling giddy. "Ma, that's a myth. You can totally fall asleep with a concussion."

"Nathan, put the nurse on, I want to speak to someone in charge."

I press the end call button and put the phone on the table beside the bed, finally letting my eyes close.

When I open them again, I'm groggy and my mouth feels like it's filled with cotton balls. Mom's sitting in the chair by my bed. She looks tired and she isn't wearing any makeup. I can't remember the last time I saw her without makeup on.

The second she sees I'm awake, she jumps to her feet.

"There you are," she says, giving me a thin smile. She brushes the hair from my forehead and strokes my head.

"Mom." I try to get up, but a searing pain shoots through my wrist and I gasp.

Mom squeals before grabbing my arm.

"Careful, Nathan. Jesus!"

Everything comes rushing back. The fight. Evan getting hurt. Me trying to help him. My wrist.

It's in one of those splint things and a wrist support. My heart sinks.

"The doctor said it's broken. You'll need a cast."

Before I can say anything, the door opens and Bryce comes in carrying a Starbucks cup. He flashes me a look I can't read before handing the drink to my mom and touching her cheek.

"Why don't you go out into the waiting room and drink

your coffee? I want to a have a quick word with Nathan." When she hesitates, he offers her a smile.

"I'll go easy on him, don't worry."

He waits until she's left the room before taking the seat and leaning forward.

"Do you know how much you've upset your mother?"

I swallow back the tears.

"She cried her eyes out all the way back from the Bahamas."

"You didn't have to come back here."

"She's your mother. Of course she wanted to come back."

I look at my wrist support and close my eyes. "If you don't care about me, what are you doing here? Is it all just for Mom?"

"Of course I care about you. I've raised you, haven't I?"

"I was already practically raised when you met her."

He scoffs. "Please. You were a kid. And even if you were already in high school, you were definitely still rough around the edges."

"I'm not some fixer-upper you can pour money into until it looks how you want it to look."

"Is that all you think I've done? Pour money into you?" He blows out a disbelieving laugh and leans back in his chair. "You might not believe it, but I care about you, Nathan. I care about you and your mother very much. I wouldn't have married her or adopted you if I didn't."

"You're not my real dad," I mutter.

"No. Where is he?"

I drop my gaze from him.

"Sorry. That was uncalled for." He sighs, running a hand over his face, his palm scratching on the stubble lining his jaw. This is probably the first time I've ever seen him unshaven. When I still lived with them, he'd even come down to breakfast fully dressed and clean-shaven, even when he didn't have to go to the office.

My voice is way smaller than I wanted it to be when I speak again. "Is Evan okay?"

His nostrils flare, but he's calm when he replies.

"He's still in the waiting room. I told him to leave. He refused until he could see you were okay."

Something warms a little inside me.

"What is it about him that you can't just turn your back on, Nathan?"

"What is it about my mom you can't turn your back on? I'm sure I've caused you more trouble than you need, but you're still here, for her."

"And for you."

"I love him."

I look up to see his reaction. He swallows, blinking.

"Does that piss you off?"

"What?"

"That I'm bi?"

He snorts. "No. You have the wrong idea about me. It's not his gender that bothers me and your mother, it's the trouble he brings into your life."

"But you know it was me who stole that car. How can you still blame him?"

"Have you been in any kind of trouble since you stopped seeing him? Until now, that is?"

I look down at my wrist in its splint. My voice is reedy when I answer. "That's because I've had opportunities he hasn't."

"Don't give me that. There are plenty of poor people who don't commit crimes-"

"Don't tell me about how you grew up with nothing again, I'm already in enough pain."

He cocks an eyebrow.

"You don't know him."

"Okay."

"He was only there the night I stole that car because I called him for help. And this." I hold the arm with the wrist support up. "He told me to get back in the car when those guys showed up, but I didn't."

Bryce's expression wavers at that. "Did they jump him because he's queer?"

"I don't know. I don't think it was just that."

Bryce takes a deep breath. "Apparently he wouldn't name them to the police."

"How do you know that?"

"Your mother spoke to his boss. If he gives us names, we can make it go away."

I snort. "Who are you? Tony Soprano?"

"I meant legally, Nathan. How many painkillers did they give you?"

"A lot."

He glances down sadly at my wrist.

"Your tennis season is over."

My heart sinks. "Yeah."

He leans over and puts his hand on my head. "You're a good kid. I just want what's best for you. That's all your mother and I want."

I have to bite back tears.

The door opens and a nurse comes in. "We're ready for you, Nathan. Time to put the cast on."

I turn to Bryce. "Can you please tell Evan I'm sorry, and make sure ... " I blush. "I don't know if he has insurance. We owe him that much, at-"

"Go with the nurse. I'll sort it."

16

EVAN

When Nate's mom came into the waiting room, she saw me and walked back out again. That was about twenty minutes ago.

I watch the window to see if I can catch Nate coming out. The nurse said he was okay, but she wouldn't give me any other information. Nate's mom and stepdad sure as shit aren't going to tell me anything.

The door opens and that guy in a fancy-ass suit comes in again. I recognized him the second I saw him from the pictures in Nate's house. He doesn't look as polished in real life.

I stand, waiting for him to punch me or something. Then I remember guys like that don't like to get their hands dirty. Maybe he'll try to buy me off or threaten my family or something. I square my shoulders.

"Stand down, son," he says.

I do as he says, instinctually, and a second later I realize why. He reminds me of those guys I'd let fuck me. Fresh shame fills me and I can barely look him in the eye.

Taking the seat opposite mine, he clasps his hands

together between his legs. He wears a simple gold wedding band. The flash of a shiny watch is visible just under his cuff.

"Nathan told me what happened."

I take in a deep breath, not trusting myself to speak.

"He's very concerned about you. Personally, I would prefer it if he had nothing to do with you ever again."

"Is he okay?"

"He has a broken wrist. His tennis season is over. Maybe his college career."

Shit. Fuck.

"But you'll still pay his tuition, right?"

A bitter smirk twists his lips.

"Yes, I'll pay his tuition. I would add the condition that he never see you again."

My stomach drops, but it's nothing I wouldn't deserve.

"Except I know he'd throw it all away for you and I don't want that."

I frown. "Nate wouldn't throw his future away. He's not stupid."

"He's not stupid. But he is in love."

My face flushes, everything in me warming up. "How do you know that?"

He shrugs. "Because he told me."

It doesn't matter, I tell myself. I can't let Nate throw everything away for me. I stand, my body aching from the fight.

"Listen, you don't have to worry. I'm not gonna bother him anymore. I knew I'd ruin his life and now I have. I just wanted to make sure he was okay, now I know he is-"

"Sit down, Evan."

I take a deep breath and do as he says.

"People told me not to marry Pamela, but I did anyway. You know why?"

"Because you're a rich guy and you can do whatever the fuck you want?"

He laughs. "No. I can't do 'whatever the fuck I want' because I have people relying on me. I have children of my own who are older but who will always be my responsibility. I have a business, employees, I have a wife, and Nathan...." he runs his fingers through his hair. I wonder if he always has this much scruff on his chin. Was he really worried about Nate? Was all that shit Nate said about him being an asshole just bullshit? Does Nate really want this guy's approval?

"I married her because I love her, and while people's concern was understandable, I know Pamela, and I trusted that she had my best interests at heart, despite what everyone said." He fixes me with an unwavering stare and I'm wondering about the point of this story. What's he expecting me to say? "Do you have Nathan's best interest at heart?"

"Yes." One hundred percent.

He nods, looking down at his hands. "You should go in and talk to him when he comes out from getting his cast."

"What about-"

He holds a hand up. "I'll talk to his mother."

He gets up. "By the way, I know I owe you a debt."

"What?"

"It was cutthroat of me to blame Nathan's little indiscretion on you."

I blink. Indiscretion? Is he talking about Nate wrapping a fucking car around a tree?

"I'd really appreciate it if you'd let me take care of the bill here."

Bill? Oh. "Fuck, no."

He laughs and shakes his head. "It's Nathan's wishes."

"I have insurance."

"I'm sure you do, but we both know it doesn't cover everything."

"I didn't even fucking need an ambulance," I mutter.

Bryce laughs again. "I know you're tough and independent, but I'm paying your bill. It's the least I can do."

He leaves before I can argue.

I poke my head around the door when I know Nate's been back for a while.

"Can I come in?"

He nods, not saying anything. He looks so fucking small and fragile in that bed. His cast on top of the sheets, weighing his arm down.

"I'm so fucking sorry, baby."

The baby just slips out. It kills me how much he lights up at it.

"Come here," he says with a soft smile. He's probably out of his mind on painkillers right now. But that smile—it kills me.

I sit down and he reaches his cast out because it's the closest arm.

"Stupid." I curse myself and shake my head, moving to the other side of the bed so he can reach me. "I just had an interesting talk with your dad."

"He's not my dad."

"Yeah, he is, Nate. He cares about you."

He drops his gaze to his cast. "What did he say?"

"He'd rather I didn't see you anymore."

"He can't-" he tries to shoot up off the bed and I press my hand gently against his chest.

"Calm down. He said he'd *rather.* But he knows how

stubborn you are and that there's nothing he can do to stop you."

He relaxes a little. "Oh."

"He said you're in love with me."

He bites his lip. "I thought that was obvious."

"Look what happened to you because of me."

"It wasn't because of you."

"It was. You'd never have run into those guys if it wasn't for me. I brought them into your life."

"And I bailed on you when you needed me most. If I'd been around, maybe you wouldn't have needed them. Maybe things would be different."

I shake my head. "Maybe. I still fucked things up for you."

"Stop it, you didn't. Bryce says you should give those guys up to the police. He says-"

"I'm not gonna do that."

"Why not?"

I loosen my grip on his hand. "Because, that's not how things work. You should know that."

"What?" He sits up, pulling his hand free. "Are you telling me you're going to still be friends with them?"

"They've never been my friends. Just people who help me move shit. I need the money."

"Evan, you can't seriously-"

I stand up. "We're up to our eyeballs in debt, Nate. We're fucking drowning and it's up to me to keep us afloat."

"I can help, I can-"

"No. Your stepdad already paid my fucking hospital bill when you're the one who got hurt trying to protect me. I won't let that happen again."

"Evan."

"Just ... rest, Nate. Get better."

"Where are you going?"

"I just need to ... I don't know."

He looks so disappointed. But looking at him lying there, I'm thinking about his stepdad grilling me in the waiting room, asking me about my intentions, telling me Nate's fucking in love with me. I'm not good enough for him. I've let him go before. After the initial sting last time, he let me go pretty easily. I'm sure he can do it again.

Nathan

It was so hard to stop myself from shaking while I laid in bed last night. My wrist throbbed under the cast. I kept forgetting about it, trying to turn over before realizing I had a cast on. I tried not to catastrophize, but it was hard not to.

Evan was right about how ignorant I am. I didn't even consider the possibility of what happened last night, not even after Evan came home that night with a bruise under his eye and a swollen nose.

My stomach roils at the memory of those guys jumping him. Standing there like an idiot, not knowing what to do, how to help him.

The way they snarled at the thought of him having a boyfriend. No wonder he's so hung up on how he feels about men.

I want more than ever to protect him, but I can't just wave a magic wand and fix everything for him. I know that now.

After spending the night at my mom and Bryce's house, I head back to the frat to face the music. Mom tried to get me to stay another day, but Bryce told her I needed to own up to my responsibilities.

"He's capable, Pamela, let him go and be a man."

I'm not sure if that was supposed to make me feel kind of proud, but it did.

It's not easy to let myself in with the key with only one working hand. I have the use of my fingers, but with the cast covering most of my hand as well as my wrist, it's still tricky trying to do things that used to be automatic.

I'm still struggling with the door when someone opens it on the other side. I stumble forward.

"Nathan, where have-" Priestley cuts himself off when he sees my wrist. "Please tell me you don't have a cast on your arm right now."

"Um ... I don't have a cast on my arm?"

"What the hell happened?"

Ben and a few of the other guys come out from the kitchen, hearing the raised voices and someone trying to get into the house.

"Shit, man, what happened to you?" Archer asks.

Before Priestley can call me out, I tell them the truth. "I got jumped."

Ben is at my side in another second, the others following closely behind. I'm bombarded with questions. *Who was it? Did you get a good look at them? Did they take anything valuable? Did you call the police? What are they doing about it?*

"Let him sit down," Priestley orders. Everyone does as he says and he leads me into the main room where we usually watch movies. I take a seat on the end of the big leather sectional and everyone gathers around me.

"I don't know who it was. I gave a description to the police. There were other witnesses, so we'll just have to wait and see."

Priestley asks the question I'd been dreading. "Where did this happen?"

"Yeah, was it on campus?" Miles asks.

"No, I was ... visiting a friend. In a different neighborhood."

"A sketchy neighborhood?" Priestley probes.

I instantly get my back up. "No, not a sketchy neighborhood. Actually, it's the neighborhood I used to live in."

"What were you doing there?"

"I just told you, I was visiting a friend."

Priestley throws a pointed glance at my wrist.

"So, I'm guessing this spells the end to your season," he says finally.

I swallow a lump in my throat. "Yeah, probably."

Everyone looks away. I have to bite the inside of my lip as a lump forms in my throat and the back of my eyes start to burn.

The guys all get ready to head out to classes, bringing their racket bags to head straight to the match later. I grab my books and laptop, fumbling only a little as I put them in my backpack. There's no point of my grabbing my racket bag, which I stare at with regret on my way out of my bedroom door.

Ben pats me on the back as we head to our business class.

"I'm sorry. Nate. This must really suck. Is Evan okay?"

I smile at him, so fucking grateful he asked. "Yeah, I think so."

"I can drive you where you need to go until your wrist heals."

"Thank you, that would actually be really helpful."

He shrugs. "Any time. That's what friends are for, right?"

I nod as I take our seats in class. Making a mental note to set Ben up with the most awesome guy on the planet if it's the last thing I do.

Thank God I have my laptop to make notes, because my

handwriting is a mess when I try to write with my left hand. After class, Ben asks me where I want to go.

"Shall I take you back to the house?"

"No way, I wanna watch you guys kick Cornell's butts."

His face lights up. "Are you sure?"

"Yep. Anyway, I'm going to need to talk to Coach Sanchez, obviously."

"Just remember, none of this is your fault. Okay?"

WHILE I WATCH my teammates play their matches from the stands, there's a lot of disappointment that I'm not out there with them, yeah. But there's something much stronger that I can't ignore, taking over everything else. And that's Evan. Evan feeling the weight of taking care of his family. Feeling like he isn't capable. Like he doesn't deserve to be happy, too. I wish I could show him how much he does deserve it. How all his mom and Stacie want is for him to be happy. To live his life.

After talking to Coach Sanchez and watching my own disappointment that my season is over mirrored on his face, I realize that this heavy feeling in my heart is nothing compared to how I feel about Evan. This was not his fault. And yes, if I'd have stayed away like he'd warned me, I wouldn't be sitting out an important match and looking at a premature end to my season. But I wouldn't have had everything that we've had over the past few weeks, either. I still wouldn't know that Evan had felt the same way about me all along. That my feelings for him weren't unrequited. And now I've had a taste of what it can be like with him, I don't want to ever let that go.

I watch the match, one eye on the scoreboard and one

on my phone, praying Evan will return my calls, a text, anything. But there's nothing.

Ben and Priestley win the doubles point together, wiping the floor with Cornell's best doubles paring. Priestley wins his singles match and Ben narrowly misses out on the W after battling it out with one of Cornell's best players. The other guys all crash out, too, and the team ends up losing the match.

I commiserate with them back at the house. Ben asking how my meeting with Coach Sanchez went. He's always so concerned about everyone else. I need to help him see that he deserves to think of himself for a change, too.

"You'll get them next time, guys."

"Nathan's right. We need to be sharp for Columbia next weekend," Priestley jumps in.

That's not what I said, but okay.

Priestley turns to me. "Have the doctors said when your wrist will be healed?"

"Probably not until after regionals," I tell him.

"That's a shame, Nathan. I would have liked to play a few last doubles matches with you before I graduate this summer."

I blink, waiting for a criticism that doesn't seem to be coming. Does Priestley Rosenthal actually like me? He sure doesn't act like it sometimes. But then, neither does Bryce—and he cut a vacation to the Bahamas short to make sure I was okay.

"Me, too."

He slaps my good hand and I excuse myself to go up to my room to be alone.

I try calling Evan again, but he doesn't pick up. I remind myself that he expects me to give up. This time, I won't.

17

EVAN

Nate only called five times today. I tell myself it's getting easier to ignore him and his messages. But I'm lying to myself.

Every time I see his name flash up on the screen, something twists in me.

I keep telling my ma and Stacie he's busy, but I'll have to break the news that he isn't coming around here anymore at some point. By that time, he will have moved on, come to his senses. Realized he has a future, and I don't. Maybe, eventually, he'll be grateful that I did him a favor and gave him an out before he ruined it all for something that's not worth it. Some*one* who isn't worth it.

Ma hands me the application form for the electrician course to hand in to Bob and I try to hide my lack of enthusiasm as she kisses me goodbye with a big smile on her face.

I thought I'd gotten used to this being my life, but now I've had a glimpse of something else, it's crushing. I look at the women around me my ma's age or older, who've been doing this for years, even decades. The men stooped from driving forklift trucks and carrying shit that was too heavy for one person. Workhorses. I don't wanna be like that. But *fuck,* what if I can't be anything else? What if Nate's wrong about me and I'm not as smart as he thinks I am? What if I flunk out of this stupid course and then I'll know for a fact, this is it? Forever?

Bob comes and finds me once I get set up. He asks me to follow him into his office. I think he's going to ask if I have the application form, but before I can pull it out of my pocket, he tells me to take a seat and I know instantly something's wrong. He's usually pretty upbeat, despite the fact that he sits in this grimy, drafty office all night, watching us sweat at the conveyor belts downstairs. But right now, he looks like someone just kicked his puppy.

"I'm so sorry to have to do this Evan, but ..."

Fuck. No. My stomach drops.

"Head office heard about the fight outside. They've told me to give you a disciplinary."

I open my mouth to say something, but Bob holds his hand up, his face apologetic.

"I know it wasn't your fault, you'd best believe I gave them a piece of my mind. I told them, we have witnesses who'll attest to the fact those thugs just jumped you. But apparently, they got wind of you not being cooperative with the police and want to make an example of you."

"What does this mean? Am I gonna lose my job?"

"No, not if I can help it."

What the fuck does that mean?

"But you gotta keep your nose clean for a while. Very clean."

"And what if those guys come back?"

Bob swallows. "You could try being more cooperative with the police. Maybe pressing charges, handing over names, addresses...."

I shake my head before he even stops speaking. "I can't do that. They know where I live. Where my ma works, where my sister goes to school...."

"Evan, if these guys are really that dangerous, then you should report them."

"It's not about that. They're just idiots. But idiots can hurt people. And I won't risk my ma and Stacie getting hurt for my stupid mistakes."

Bob frowns and clasps his hands over his belly. "What do you mean? What mistakes?"

I shake my head. This guy is my boss. I can't tell him half of what I've done. I'd be fired on the spot if he ever found out I brought anything illegal into the warehouse. He sits up with a sigh, letting his hands drop. "Evan, I'm going to do everything I can. I know how much you need this job. And I know your mother. I know how tough your dad's death has been on you all, and his illness ... "

I try to tune his voice out. Anyone talking about my dad feels like nails being drilled into my head. I thought I'd gotten so good at tuning it out—but it's so loud right now. It feels like everything is closing in on me. Like I'm letting my dad down. Letting my ma and Stacie down. If he were here, if he'd never gotten sick, he wouldn't have let us get to this point. He'd make it better. He could fix anything....

"Evan? Are you okay? You look a little pale."

"I'm fine." I shake my head, the world coming back in sudden, vivid clarity. "I'll keep my nose clean. You're right, I really need this job."

I'm not even thinking about the application form until I'm about to leave the office and Bob calls me back. That apologetic look on his face is even more intense now.

"What is it?"

"I'm afraid you'll have to hold out on applying for the

electrician course. Employees under disciplinary action aren't allowed to apply for education and training programs."

I tense my jaw. "It's fine," I say through gritted teeth.

"You can apply once your disciplinary's gone through … " I turn around and leave before I can say something I might regret, rushing to the bathroom before anyone can stop me.

I feel like screaming. I need to hit something. I pull the form out of my pocket instead. Glance at the questions I spent ages answering at the kitchen table last night while Ma hovered excitedly around me, pretending to wash dishes while peering over my shoulder and reminding me of all my good qualities. The action of ripping it to pieces is satisfying at first. I rip it until its unrecognizable and then kick the pieces under my heavy boots. But it's not enough.

When Ivan—the forklift truck driver—comes in I'm in the process of bloodying my knuckles on the stall door. I stop what I'm doing. He studies me for a second and then walks over to the urinal and starts taking a piss. Blood trickles over my knuckles while I stand there, panting, waiting for him to leave.

"Want me to help you tidy up in here?" he asks, gesturing to the pieces of application form shredded all over the dirty tiles.

I shake my head. If I try to speak right now, I'm gonna cry. And that's the last thing I need.

Ivan shrugs before heading back out onto the floor. I take a shaky breath before bending down to pick up my mess.

THE FIRST FEW times I walked out of work after leaving Nate that day, I kept expecting to find his SUV parked up when I came out the back door. I told myself I was relieved when I didn't, but my heart sinks when I don't find it here now.

I'm doing the right thing, I remind myself. *Nate deserves so much better than what you can give him.*

But fuck me, I could do with seeing him right now. More than ever. And yet, I'm even more of a loser now than I was a week ago, two weeks ago. Five years ago.

MA'S still up when I get home. She's sitting at the kitchen table and I swear I smell cigarette smoke in the air.

She looks tired. Dark rings around her eyes. She glances up at me when I walk into the room.

"What are you still doing up? It's late."

"Sorry, Ma," she says, flashing me a weak smile.

I sit down at the table and put my hand out to her and she squeezes it with both of hers.

"How did it go tonight? Did you hand the form in with Bob?"

I swallow the lump in my throat and grit my teeth before lying to her. "Yeah."

That smile that ghosts over her lips almost sets me off. I bite the inside of my lip so hard it hurts.

"I'm so proud of you, baby."

Fuck, stop.

"I love you, so much," she says, pulling her hand out from under mine to stroke my face. "Your dad would be so proud of how you're keeping everything together."

"Stop it, Ma." I pull away from her touch and stand up with a harsh scrape of my chair legs on the vinyl floor.

"What's wrong? What's happened?"

"Nothing's happened, everything's fine, Ma." I swipe at

my face so she can't see that a few stray tears have escaped. "I just don't wanna talk about Dad, that's all."

"Evan, baby, you've got to talk about him sometime. It'll drive you crazy if you keep it all bottled up. You don't have to be strong all the time. Your dad wasn't strong all the time."

I spin on my heels, a muscle ticking in my jaw. "Yeah, he was."

She cocks her head. I can't stand the sympathy in her eyes. "Evan, your dad was a man. He was human. He wouldn't expect you to be anything other than that."

Memories of a big man in blue overalls flood to the surface. The smell of his woody cologne and cigarette smoke on his clothes. The warmth of his chest when he'd pull me in for a hug. My chest aches. I can't look at her anymore. My gaze flits over the table. A pile of new letters. An envelope with a big red banner.

"Is that another final reminder?"

Ma makes a feeble attempt to cover the letters up without looking to see what she's doing.

"Don't worry about that. We'll figure it out."

She stands, running her hand over my head before putting her arms around me. I'm stiff as she rests her head on my shoulder. Her familiar perfume overpowered by a strong smell of smoke and something chemical, like gin or vodka.

"Get some sleep, okay? I love you."

"You too, Ma. Go to bed."

There's a lump in my throat as she leaves. I try to make a sandwich before bed, but I'm not hungry anymore. I put the knife down mid-spread and hold onto the counter for support while waiting for all the memories threatening to break through to pass.

I'm about to turn my phone off when it lights up with

another message from Nate. It's late and I can't sleep, and I know the later it gets, the stronger the desire to call him is. The weaker my resistance. My thumb hovers over the last message as I read the start:

I'm not giving up on you. Not this time, I'm never...

I turn my phone off, shoving it under the pillow before turning over to try and get some sleep.

I DON'T THINK anyone's in the kitchen when I come downstairs the next morning, but then I hear Ma, swearing to herself from somewhere.

"Shit, shit, shit, shit, shit!"

"What's happened?"

She's on the floor, her head in the cupboard under the sink.

"Sink's leaking," she says.

"Here, let me take a look."

"It's no good," she says, getting up and wiping the dust off her knees.

I crouch down to where she was, the vinyl still warm. Sticking my head under the sink, I catch the smell of bleach and something damp and musty. There's a big crack in the u-bend of the pipe that takes the sink water out into the drain.

"We'll have to call a plumber," she says.

"We can't afford a plumber."

"Well, what are we supposed to do? We need a sink, Ev."

"I'll fix it."

She raises an eyebrow.

"I know how to do it, Dad taught me."

She swallows and I look away, not wanting to catch the emotion on her face.

"The tools are in the garage. Do you think you can fight your way in?"

"Yeah, I'll sort it."

The garage is a fucking mess. No one's been in here for years and I have to fight just to get past the door, stubbing my toe on old mildewing boxes. Looking inside everything to try and find the blue toolbox I remember Dad going around the house, fixing shit with. Most of the stuff in the boxes is old crap, like Stacie's headless dolls and school projects Ma refuses to throw out.

There are boxes of photo albums, too. I put them to one side without looking too closely.

Old car parts are stuffed behind the boxes. Most of them rusted and no use to anyone but the junk yard guy. I make a pile of those outside the garage to take to the junk yard, maybe try and sell them as scrap metal.

Ma brings me a sandwich and a glass of Coke at lunchtime and I sit on a box and wolf it down before getting back to work. Dad always warned me how important momentum is. How hard it is to get back into something once you take a break. I push out thoughts of him in here, fixing up cars before he got sick, and carry on with my work. But I can't help it. Being in here, surrounding by all this stuff. It has him all over it.

I force myself to focus. It's a task. These are just things. They have no real importance. They're in the way of me fixing the sink, that's all.

I finally find the toolbox, hiding behind another stack of damp cardboard boxes. I recognize the dark blue color right away. Crouching down, I wipe the dust and grime off it and something catches in my chest at the familiar writing in black Sharpie. My breathing is ragged, I can hear it in my ears, along with a rush, like the ocean, pouring in.

This is my writing. I did it when I was about six years old. Helping Dad fix something around the house. Looking up at him like he was the fucking moon and stars. It says:

Evan and Dad.

That's it. Evan and Dad. Just two words. *Fuck.*

I have to sit down. My hand rests on the toolbox, like it's gonna disappear if I let go. Everything forces its way to the surface. Every scrap I've been holding back behind some invisible wall. It all comes crashing down at once. Every memory I've ever had of my dad seems to seep out. Him teaching me and Nate to ride our bikes on this very street. How he'd dive on the ground so we fell on him instead of the hard concrete, to stop us from hurting ourselves. How he took us to the bike store as a reward and bought us any bell we wanted. I chose Mickey Mouse and Nate chose Ninja Turtles.

I remember sitting on his shoulders at the Fourth of July firework display in the park. His soft hair under my hands, the smell of Marlboros on his fingers. The way I'd sleep in his flannel shirts when he was away. The way he'd make a beeline for me when he came home from work and sweep me up in his arms. How I'd follow him around and how he didn't mind. I'd sit in the passenger seat of his work van and play with the stereo with the broken dials. Sometimes I'd just sit out in the van on the driveway and pretend I was him, on my way to work. I'd see him peek out of the window every now and then and smile.

He was my world and I had to watch him slowly disappear before he finally left us forever. I was too scared to be there most of the time. It hurt to see a faded version of him, but he never made me feel bad about it. And now I've let him down. I've failed him. He told me it was my job to take care of my ma and Stacie, and I've failed in the last thing he asked me to do for him.

Nathan

When calling doesn't work, I take the initiative to go over there and talk to Evan face to face. Maybe I'll have to start over? Build up from *Go back to your frat bros, Nate,* to *You can come in until Ma gets home.*

It felt weird to ask Ben to drive me to my old neighborhood, but when he asked where I was going, he insisted on taking me.

When he pulls up outside Evan's house, the garage is open and Old Tom is looking through the blinds next door. And crouched in a ball in the open garage, surrounded by piles of boxes and old car parts, is Evan.

I know something's wrong straight away. Something about the way he's balled up like that.

"Is that Evan?" Ben asks.

"You can go back to the house, if you want."

"Are you sure? I can wait. If you guys need a ride somewhere...."

I squeeze his shoulder and he trails off. "Thank you, but I can take it from here."

I get out of the car, and when I get closer, I see Evan's got his hand on something. Closer still, I recognize it as his dad's blue toolbox. We used to play in it as kids. Used to watch his dad fixing things around the house and pretend to be him. His dad let him draw on it with crayons. A sharpie.

I crouch down beside him. If he's crying, he's doing it quietly.

"Ev?"

His shoulders shake a little. I put my hand between his shoulder-blades and spread my fingers. He's cold.

"How long have you been out here?"

He doesn't answer.

I press my forehead to the side of his head and hear him sniffle while I rub his back. "I'm here."

He starts crying, his shoulders shaking. The sound destroys me. I would do anything to never hear Evan cry again. Anything to take his pain away.

When he pulls his arm away, his face is covered in tears, his eyes red and his cheeks blotchy.

His voice is raw when he says, "I miss my dad."

It's like a gut punch. I can hear the pure emotion in it. The pain.

"I know. I miss him, too." My stomach swoops uncomfortably. I've been pushing out how much I miss Joe, the grief I haven't felt the right to feel. But seeing Evan curled up and in pain like that, I realize more than ever that I understand. Years may have passed, but we're still connected by so many things. There were threads between us that were always going to be impossible to break.

He looks at me. At first, it's like he can't see me. Like he's lost in his own world of grief. But then his eyes focus and he sees me, really sees me.

"I know you do. I'm sorry, Nate."

He rests his head against mine and I put my arms around him, letting him cry. Soothing him as best I can.

"I was a coward."

"What? No, you weren't."

He nods. "I was scared to see him like that in the end, I stayed away. He probably thought I didn't care."

"No way. Your dad knew how much you loved him."

He sniffles and wipes his face with the back of a grimy arm.

"I never said goodbye, you know?" He looks at me with such pain in his eyes, every instinct tells me to look away, but I force myself to hold his gaze. "I knew he was dying, and I couldn't bring myself to do it."

"He understood, Ev."

"I know. That makes it worse. I should have said goodbye. I wish...."

He trails off. I rub his back.

"I should have said goodbye to my dad."

I don't even know what to say to that. I don't think there's anything I *can* say that would make the slightest bit of difference. So I just say what I do know.

"I'm not gonna tell you it'll get better, because I don't know that. But I am here. And so is your mom, and Stacie, and your dad was loved, and that's all that matters."

He puts his forehead on mine and I keep looking in his eyes while I wipe his tears away with my thumb.

I hear a car pull up. Evan must hear it too, but he doesn't move, so neither do I.

Someone clears their throat. When they speak, I recognize Theresa's voice. "Everything okay in here?"

"Yeah," Evan says without taking his eyes off me.

She pauses. She's hesitant when she speaks again, unsure. "Okay, well ... come in for dinner when you're ready. It's cold out here."

Evan smiles a little. "Thank you," he whispers to me as his mom heads into the house.

"What for?"

"Being here."

"Of course I'm here. It's where I belong."

When we go inside, Theresa's setting up the table in the kitchen and the smell of pizza floats from the oven.

She looks up uncertainly at Evan, then me. "Everything okay?"

Even's eyes and nose are red from crying. I expect him to bristle. To push her away. Pretend he didn't break down.

Instead, he steps around me and puts his arms around her. She squeezes him so tightly her knuckles turn white as she grips his shirt. He clears his throat after a minute and she rubs his back before they break away.

"I'm okay, Ma. You okay?"

She wipes her face. "I'm good. Pizza's almost ready."

"Good, I'm starving."

Theresa looks past Evan, giving me a grateful smile.

We're quiet as we sit down to eat. Evan chewing cautiously, though he'd told his mom he was starving. I know he's just trying to make her feel better. Stop her from worrying.

"I found the toolbox."

She looks up. "Oh? Ev, don't worry about the sink, we'll-"

"I'll fix it. Nate'll help. Right, Nate?"

"Huh? Oh, yeah, of course."

"It was a shit hole in there," Evan says. "Found all kinds of stuff we should throw out. Decapitated Barbies mostly."

Theresa laughs. "I wasn't sure if Stacie would want them or not."

"No one wants that, Ma." Evan grins and she visibly relaxes a little.

He goes quiet, running his crust over some tomato sauce on the plate. "Ma, what did Dad think about people being gay?"

As he asks the question, he keeps looking at the plate, squishing the crust harder against it.

I watch her, watching him so intensely I think she's going to burn a hole in the side of his face. "Your father wasn't homophobic," she says, her voice somehow both gentle and rock solid. "He wouldn't have stood for that shit."

He swallows. She reaches over, puts her hand on one of his.

"Wanna know something else?"

"Hm?"

"Your father loved you. More than *anything*. And he would be so proud of you, Evan."

She turns her gaze on me and I look down. "Both of you."

Evan looks up, nostrils flaring, defiance in his eyes. "I can't apply for that course. I lied to you." His jaw is clenched.

"Why not?"

"I got a disciplinary at work, because of the fight."

"That's not fair!" Theresa takes the words right out of my mouth.

"Evan, we can fight this," I say.

He shakes his head. "Bob said he won't let me lose my job. He thinks I should give the guys who jumped us up to the cops."

"You should," Theresa says.

Evan shakes his head. "They know where we live."

"So what?"

"They'll terrorize you and Stace. No, Ma, you won't convince me to do that."

"So what? They just get away with it?"

"If I give them up, they'll get community service, maybe a little jail time. Then they'll be out there, doing it again. This time, it'll be you and Stacie. I promised Dad I'd look out for you both."

"I'll give them up."

They both look at me.

"I went to school with them, too. I know their names. And it's me who got injured. I could even threaten to sue them, scare them off coming after you guys. Let me use Bryce's connections for something good for once."

Theresa smiles. "I think that's a good idea."

"I think you should stay out of it."

"Evan!"

"No Ma, I won't let Nate get hurt again. No fucking way."

I soften. He keeps his eyes on me.

I put my hand on the table, heart pounding in my ears as I wait to see if he'll take it in front of his mom. He does.

"You don't have to take care of everyone all the time, Ev. It's okay sometimes to let people take care of you."

He drops his gaze, looks down at our hands clasped on the table.

"Nate's right." Theresa says. She leans closer and plants a kiss on top of my head as she stands.

"Make sure you two get some sleep. I'll see you both in the morning."

We crawl into bed, both too exhausted to do anything but sleep. I have classes in the morning and Evan has work. There's so much to unpack, but I know he's fragile right now. We need to take everything one step at a time.

18

NATHAN

Seeing as they had to cut their Bahamas vacation short, my mom and Bryce decided to go to Martha's Vineyard for a few weeks once they've seen I'm fine and my arm isn't going to fall off, so I have the house to myself again.

I brought Evan over last night to give him some space from his house. With all those freshly cracked open memories of his dad, he seems exhausted by the onslaught of emotion. When we got back here, he crawled into bed and slept like a baby in my arms.

I left him napping still while I left for class this morning. Since I don't have tennis practice, I get back to the house early. I let myself in and call Evan's name, walking around the first floor, panic rising when he doesn't answer. I head upstairs, checking my room first. He's still in bed. He opens his eyes when he hears me come in.

"Were you still asleep?" I ask, sitting on the edge of the bed.

"No, I just lay here for a bit."

I run my good hand over his shaved head, remembering

that nice, blond hair he used to have when we were kids. Try not to focus on the bruises under his eyes and the new cut healing on his top lip.

He looks up at me and our eyes meet. My chest feels so tight I can barely breathe.

"What?" he asks. "What's wrong?"

"I just love you so much."

He blinks at me with those blue eyes and my heart thuds in my chest. I want him to say it back, but I tell myself it's hard for him, and I don't need him to, not right now.

"Come 'ere."

I shake my head, tracing my thumb over the pattern his freckles make on his cheeks.

"No?"

I smile. "Make me," I say, moving my thumb over his lips. *Fuck, I love these lips.* No one on earth has lips like Evan. Just looking at them causes the pit of my stomach to fizz.

He pulls me by the arm, careful not to bump my cast, until I'm on top of him.

"Made you," he says with a soft smile.

I hold his face in my good hand so I can control the kiss. Brushing my lips slowly and gently over his. He clamps his mouth shut and I lean back.

"What's wrong?"

"Does my breath stink?"

"No, it doesn't. And I wouldn't care if it did."

I brush my lips against his again, coaxing him slowly to open up. Finally, he gives in, his body sagging and letting go. He sighs into my mouth as our tongues meet and I grind my hips automatically against his.

"I've never wanted anyone the way I want you," I whisper into his mouth.

He sighs and closes his eyes.

"I love you."

"You're gonna kill me," he says.

I kiss him again, feeling his hands roam over my back down to my ass.

He flips us over, rips the blanket from between us and throws it to the floor. He's half naked, in nothing but some Calvin Klein boxer briefs.

"Are these mine?" I ask, amused.

"Yeah. Take this off." He tugs at my polo, helping me pull it off over my head.

"You don't have to be careful with me, you know? My arm doesn't hurt at all, and the cast keeps it safe."

He drops his gaze, tracing a finger over the hard surface of the cast. "I know. I just fucking hate that you got hurt. Wish I could get them back for you."

"I already told you, I'm going to give them up. They'll be punished for what they did."

"I wasn't talking about the cops."

I grab the back of his neck and pull his face closer, my heart thumping in my ears. "Don't you dare do something you'll get in trouble for. I don't want you getting hurt either."

His jaw untenses and that line between his eyebrows smooths itself out as his face relaxes. "Okay, I won't."

"Promise me."

"I promise."

"Good. Now, come here."

His skin is clammy and warm. He smells the way he used to smell when we'd spend all day playing video games in his bed. I drag my good hand over his back and find his ass through his underwear. He groans into my mouth.

"Evan."

"Yeah?"

"Let me suck your cock. Please?"

"*Fuck*." He laughs, letting go of my arm with the cast, where he has it pinned protectively to my side before lying down beside me. "Have I told you you're gonna kill me?"

"A couple of times."

He hesitates. "I need a shower."

"I don't care." My heart pounds at the thought of his smell. I need to get close to it. Need it, need *him* to consume me.

I drag my lips over his neck and chest, taking his St. Christopher between my teeth while he watches.

His nipples pebble under my tongue as I lavish attention on each one. He's hard, his cock pressing against my stomach as I make my way down. I lick his bellybutton and he flinches.

"Argh, don't do that."

I look up.

"Does that feel weird?"

"Yeah, leave it alone."

I laugh. "Okay."

I lick a stripe from just under his bellybutton to the waistband of my boxers. It turns me on so much that he's wearing them, even if he did get them clean from the drawer.

I leave the shorts on as I brush my lips over the waist-band, down to the soft cotton covering his cock and balls. I bury my face in it, inhaling his scent. He hisses and lets out a groan. *God, I want to make him feel good.*

He buries his hand in my hair and his hips buck, though I can tell he's trying to keep them still. I drag my lips over his hard length, still under the fabric, my own cock straining to be set free. I tongue him through the cotton, greedy for his musky smell. My tongue finds the head and I wrap my lips around it, the fabric already damp.

His voice, when he speaks, is so fucking hot. Hoarse and breathless.

"Take them off, please Nate, *fuck*."

I yank the waistband and his cock springs free. On my knees, I watch him, naked and splayed out on my bed, looking so good it hurts.

"If you're gonna just sit there looking at me, at least give me something to look at," he says, the need seeping out through his voice.

My face heats up as I unzip my chinos and pull them down to my knees, my boxer briefs following close behind. Evan's gaze falls on my cock, swollen and leaking already just from the sight of him.

It feels weird with my left hand when I grip the base tight and start stroking myself, but I'm distracted by the way Evan licks his lips and slides his hand down his stomach until he's stroking his cock, watching me.

I nudge his knee with my casted hand and he slides his legs wider and plants his feet. His balls hang tight over his taint. And, *fuck*, his ass looks so good.

His gaze is locked on me as he strokes himself, smearing pre-cum over his shaft, hips bucking off the bed.

I need to touch him. I can't hold off any longer. I shuffle closer and bend down to catch his lips with mine.

"I can't believe I get to have you like this."

"You talk a lot," he says with a cheeky smile.

"You love it."

"Yeah, I do," he replies without hesitation.

"Ev?"

He lets out a contented hum.

"I want you to fuck me."

I don't let him stop the kiss when he hesitates. "Please."

He flattens his legs on the bed and hooks his hands under my thighs, pulling them apart so I'm straddling him.

"You take control."

My pulse quickens. "I don't know what I'm doing."

"I'll show you."

He reaches behind him and takes the lube from my drawer, squeezing some out on his hand. He slides it past my balls, finding my crack and sliding his fingers between my cheeks until he's circling my hole.

No one has ever touched me here before. I've thought about it. Heard guys saying it feels good when their girlfriends do it, but I've never been brave enough to try. But I trust Evan, more than anything. I give myself over to it, to him. Let him do whatever he wants to me.

The tip of his index finger presses against my entrance.

"You sure about this?"

"Mm." I nod. "I've heard how you moan when I fuck you. I wanna know what that feels like."

He pushes his finger in about an inch and I start to press back on it.

His voice is so sexy when he speaks. "Want me to make you moan?"

"Mm."

He presses his finger in deeper, the stretch turning into a burn.

I force myself to sit back on it. When he adds another I let out something between a moan and a yelp.

"Slow." Evan warns. He comes up on his elbow and kisses me. Pausing with his fingers until I start wriggling on them. Pressing all the way to the knuckles and brushing against something inside me that feels so good, I let out another yelp. Evan grins.

"That feel good?"

"Fuck, what was that?"

"Your prostate." He presses again, stroking and massaging in a way that makes me want to simultaneously tell him to stop and do it again.

I flop against him, exhausted already.

"I don't think I'll last with your cock in me."

He laughs softly while planting kisses on my neck.

"I don't think I should put my cock in you yet."

"Why not?"

"Because you're not ready."

"I am."

"You're not. You're so tight, I'm gonna hurt you if I fuck you."

"I don't care." I grasp the back of his head, pulling him in closer.

"I do. The first time I got fucked, it hurt. I don't want that for you."

My stomach drops. Thinking about him being used by other men. Men who never cared about him the way he deserves to be cared about. "Evan ... "

"Come 'ere."

He lies back, taking his fingers out of me, maneuvering me up the bed until my knees are planted on the pillow either side of his head.

"What are you ... "

"Like that."

"What do you want me to ... "

Evan takes my cock in his mouth and starts sucking while he watches me.

My whole body shivers and I give in to it. The expression on his face softens, his wide eyes relaxing. I don't move at first. He bobs his head up off the bed to suck me deep before pulling off.

"You can move. I'm gonna get a sore neck doing it like this."

"Sorry."

He smiles. "Just do what feels good, okay?"

I nod. "Okay."

He rests his head back on the pillow and I move my hips until the head of my cock is brushing his lips. He lifts his head up a little and then relaxes it again when I inch deeper into his mouth. I take my time, being careful. Evan wraps his arms around my waist and pulls me in deeper, gripping my ass.

We moan at the same time as I get fully seated, gripping the headboard for support.

I watch his face carefully as I rock my hips, slowly, carefully fucking his mouth. Apart from his eyes watering, I don't see anything to suggest I'm choking him. He's taking it easily, so I keep rocking. The feeling is unbelievable. Then his hand slides closer to my crack and his fingers are probing again. His lubed-up fingers finding my hole and circling it.

I bite my lip as I rock my hips, pushing back onto his fingers before pushing forward into his mouth.

I let him in. He brushes that spot every time I pull off so I can get deeper into his mouth. My head swims with everything he's making me feel. I think about how consumed by me he must be, my smell, my taste.

His free hand slides over my thigh.

"Squeeze if you're okay," I tell him.

He gives my thigh a tight squeeze and I let go, rutting

against his fingers, unable to decide what I want more, his fingers or his mouth.

I decide. Pulling out of his mouth and sitting back on his fingers. Tears have left a trail down the sides of his face. His lips are swollen.

"Do you think I'm ready for your cock now?"

He nods.

I take the condoms out and slide one over his erection. Lubing him up before maneuvering myself over him.

"Go slow, Nate. Don't try to take more than you can."

I nod, sitting back until his head is lined up with my hole. I bite my lip as I inch down, feeling his head press against my entrance. There's resistance at first. A little burn. Then he's inside.

My heart races and I try not to be overwhelmed by what's happening. Evan is inside me. I'm about to get fucked for the first time right now. By Evan.

"Okay, Nate?"

"Yeah, you?"

He smiles. "Yeah."

I dip lower, his cock sinking deeper inside me. The burn gets worse, and then it's more than a burn, more like a sharp pain.

I stop with a gasp.

"Stay there."

I nod. I don't think I could move if I tried.

Evan coats his palm with lube and starts stroking my cock.

I watch him, watch his hand moving, his face while he stares at me, his lips parted. He wants me. *Fuck, that's so hot.* My body relaxes as Evan makes me feel good and I sink down little further before meeting that resistance again and sliding up.

"Oh!"

Wow, okay, that feels good. I do it again. Pulling out a little before sinking back down to the spot before it starts to hurt. Evan stops stroking my cock to grip my hips, tight, while I keep riding him slowly.

I stroke myself when I get close to the pain and keep fucking myself on Evan's cock. The more I move, the easier this gets. The less it hurts.

"That's it, Nate," he says, encouraging me. "*Fuck*, that's it."

I start to roll my hips, sink deeper and deeper every time I come down.

A flush spreads up Evan's chest to his neck and cheeks.

"You look so hot right now," I say.

"Fuck Nate, you're fucking perfect."

It stops hurting. Only when I sink down until our skin slaps is there still a slight sting, but holy fuck is it worth it.

"Oh god, this feels good!"

Evan smiles. "Told you."

I grip the back of his neck. "Does it feel good for you too?"

"Fuck yeah. Don't stop."

I press against his chest, urging him to relax, his hands on my hips while I ride him.

I feel possessed as I dig my fingers into Evan's skin. When he sees it's not hurting, he starts to buck his hips and meet me in the middle until we find a rhythm and ride like crazy, grunting and moaning and saying all kinds of crazy half sentences about how hot we find each other and how good it feels.

"Gonna come," I say, feeling myself start to tip over the edge.

"Come."

Evan's voice is enough to send me over the edge. I sit up and jerk myself frantically with my good hand while Evan takes control, bucking his hips up to fuck me until I'm spilling over my fingers, shooting all over Evan's chest with a shout.

He lifts me and pulls me against him while I catch my breath. The warmth of his body and the solidity of his chest is so soothing, I could fall asleep like this.

I look up and he smiles.

"Hey, you good?"

I nod. "Mmm."

His laugh vibrates through me.

"That was so good."

He laughs.

"I know. You were so fucking good at it."

Panic jolts my head up. "You didn't come."

"Don't worry about it."

I climb off him, his cock still hard, wrapped in the condom.

He kicks his legs off the bed and snaps it off.

"Evan."

"I told you don't-"

"Come back here so I can suck your cock."

Me from a few months ago might have blushed hearing myself say something like that. But not current me. Not with Evan.

He just smiles softly. "I'll be right back," he says.

While he's gone, my head swims with worries. What if the condom wasn't clean? What if he thought I was bad at it?

I'm sitting on the bed looking down at my knees when he comes back in.

"Hey, what's up?" he crouches between my knees.

"Was I bad at it?"

"I told you. You were fucking amazing."

He kisses my cheek before moving onto my neck. "Who knew golden boy Nate Castellani would take cock like a pro his first time?"

I soften.

"You're the only person who calls me that."

"Calls you what? A cock whore?"

I laugh and slap his chest. "No, Castellani. My mom changed my name to Carter. She won't even call me Nate anymore."

"Which one do you prefer?" His face is so close to mine. I could count the freckles spread across his nose and cheeks if he let me.

"I prefer whatever you call me."

He presses his forehead against mine. "Told you, you're gonna kill me."

"I love you."

He squeezes his eyes shut. "You shouldn't."

"Well, I do, so deal with it. You don't have to say it back, I-"

"*Fuck*, Nate." He stands up, his body is so beautiful. The S-shape his hips make, the V-shape leading into his groin. His erection has softened into a semi. I want to change that.

"You know I fucking love you. Always have. Stop teasing me with what I shouldn't want," he says.

Everything inside me fizzles at his admission. I reach for his hand and take in a shuddery breath when he gives it to me.

"You have me, I'm here. There's no getting rid of me this time."

He looks down at me like he's seeing me for the first time.

He pulls me up and puts his arms around me, holding me tight. I rest my head on his shoulder and let him stroke my back.

"Promise me something?"

"Anything."

"You're so stupid for a smart guy. You don't even know what you're agreeing to."

I laugh.

"Promise me that if this thing between us starts to mess up what you've got here and at school and everything—your future—you'll tell me so I can walk away."

"Evan-"

"No. No excuses, that's my condition. If you promise me that, I promise I'll go with it. I'll just fucking enjoy whatever this is, for as long as you want it. But I can only do that if I know I'm not ruining your life."

"Evan, of course you're not ruining my-"

"Nate," he says in a warning tone.

I take a deep breath, inhaling the mild scent of fresh sweat on his skin.

"I'll promise on one condition," I say.

"You don't get to negotiate here."

"It's just a small thing, I promise."

He hesitates before answering. "Okay, what is it?"

"I'll tell you if you're ruining my life, if you come back to bed with me and let me make you come."

He snorts. "Jesus, Nate, you've got a one-track mind."

I shrug. "That's my condition."

He pulls away and frowns into my face. "I'm serious, Nate."

"So am I."

He raises an eyebrow.

"*I* am," I insist, taking his hand in mine. "I know you are, and I'm being serious when I say I promise."

I can promise him this, because I know he won't ruin my life, he could only ever make it better. None of that other stuff matters without him. I know that for a fact because I've lived the last five years of my life learning it.

He leans back in and kisses me, slow and tender.

"Deal."

19

NATHAN

Stacie opens the front door when I knock.

There's laughter coming from the living room. It sounds like Evan and his mom.

I follow Stacie inside. They're on the rug in the living room, photographs spread out in front of them. They both look up and smile when they see me come in.

"Hey what's going on?"

Theresa keeps sorting through the photographs while she answers. "We're looking for pictures for a frame I got, you know those collage ones? Come help us, Nate."

I take a seat next to Evan and kiss his cheek. Stacie giggles and Theresa grins.

The photographs spread out on the floor look like they span decades. Some of them are a bit faded and raggedy around the edges.

"I'm trying to sort them, but these two keep messing them up," Evan complains.

Stacie and Theresa share a conspiratorial giggle and Evan rolls his eyes.

"Hey, Nate, here's one of you." Stacie shoves a picture under my nose and I take it from her.

"There's loads of you, Nate. I sorted some into a pile there for you to look at."

I thank her and start looking at the pictures.

The huge stack shows me at various stages of life, between the ages of around three and twelve. Always with Evan. Usually grinning, like we've just got up to mischief, or are about to.

"Look at you two in this one," Theresa says, handing me a more recent one, where we must be about fourteen.

"You're looking at Evan like he hung the moon."

"Not much has changed there."

Evan groans. "Will you two stop?"

I laugh. Theresa's looking at me like *I* hung the moon.

"Here, Ma, this is a good one." Evan slides her a picture of us all outside the house. Evan and I are around ten years old. Evan's bike with the shiny Mickey Mouse bell is leaning against the garage door and Evan's dad's work van is parked up on the driveway. Evan's dad looks healthy. He's smiling, so is Theresa. Stacie is a toddler in a stroller. For once, she isn't crying.

"Yeah, that is a good one," Theresa says, looking at it like she's back in the moment, living it.

We help her put the chosen pictures in her collage frame and hang it on the living room wall with some tools from Evan's dad's toolbox.

Evan and I finish sorting the photographs, laughing about our hairstyles or clothes or the poses we pulled, thinking we were cool. I leave Evan to put them in the right albums and go out to help Theresa with the dishes.

She smiles when she sees me, looking less tired than the last time I saw her.

"I'm glad you're here," she says, running a hand through my hair.

"Me, too."

She starts washing the dishes and I pick the towel up and stand beside her while she hands me the clean plates to dry.

"Thank you," she says.

"No problem."

"I don't mean for this. I mean for what you've done for him."

I swallow. "Theresa, there's something you should know."

"What is it?"

"It was my fault, back then. The car thing. Evan was just trying to help me, he didn't steal that car."

Her hands pause in the soapy water and my blood runs cold while I imagine her throwing me out. Was I wrong to tell her? I've told Evan so many times I want to, but he wouldn't let me.

"I didn't say anything, but my stepdad and the lawyer were trying to protect me. I swear, if I could go back and change it I...."

She takes her hands out of the water and dries them on a dish towel before putting them on my face. "You were a kid. He protected you. Did you see how many of those family photos you were in? You're a part of this family, too. Just don't go getting into any more trouble, do you hear?"

I let out a sigh of relief. "Yes, Ma."

She ruffles my hair before turning back to the dishes. "Anyway, you've more than made up for it now. Getting him away from those losers. You know I saw a few of them picking litter up on the sidewalk the other day. Community service I guess."

I snort. When I glance sideways at her, she looks years younger than she did when I first saw her again at the funeral.

When we head back into the living room, Evan and Stacie are laughing at a picture of her dressed in a Santa Claus outfit their dad took from the dancing Santa doll they used to display in the window.

"This is child abuse!" she wails.

Evan looks up with a smile and catches my eye. "Hey Stace, let me steal Nate for a minute, k?" She sighs dramatically, like she's bothered, but she goes back to sorting the pictures.

He takes me upstairs by the hand, closing the door behind us.

"You know we can't have sex with your mom and Stacie downstairs."

"Such a dirty mind," he tuts, shaking his head. "I wanted to show you something."

He reaches to the back of the old bookcase and takes a couple of DVD cases out, opening one. When he gets closer, I see that it's the case for *GTA: Vice City.* I thought maybe he'd lost this one, because every time I come over, we play *San Andreas.* Or I play *NHL 09* with Stacie and laugh at the terrible graphics while getting my ass handed to me by a thirteen-year old.

"Oh cool, you found it."

"Smell it."

He sticks it under my nose and I wince. "*Gah*, that stinks of weed."

"This is where I kept my stash."

"Okay?"

"It's empty. I'm not doing that shit anymore."

He puts the case down on the table beside the bed and takes a seat next to me. "That financial plan your friend Ben worked out is gonna help us pay off our debts in the next five years, if I'm sensible, which I will be. It means I can stay away from all that shit that got me into trouble, that got *you* hurt."

"Evan, how many times do I have to tell you it wasn't your fault? And those dicks are being punished for it. I just wish they could be punished for what they did to you, too."

He drops his gaze, like this wasn't the reaction he expected and I realize he's showing me this empty weed stash so I can be happy for him. Or so I can see that he's changed. But I already knew that. I take his hand.

"I'm proud of you."

"Psht, I don't need you to say that."

"Yeah, but you want me to."

He laughs, shaking his head.

I lean in to kiss him when the door swings open.

"Jesus, don't you knock?" Evan throws a pillow at the door, but Stacie blocks with her incredible reflexes.

"Ma said you two better hadn't be doing anything she wouldn't do up here."

Evan snorts. "What does that even mean? Get out of my room."

"Hey, don't talk to her like that."

Stacie puffs her chest out when I defend her. It's our little thing.

"You don't understand what it's like to be siblings. This is our love language, isn't it Stace?"

"No, you're just a dick." She slams the door with a big grin on her face before another pillow comes flying at her.

"That was childish."

"Yeah well, you're in love with me, so what does that say about you?"

I push him back on the bed. But like she's got x-ray eyes or something, Stacie shouts through the door, "I mean it! No hanky panky in there!"

"Oh great, I don't think my dick's ever gonna get hard again."

I pretend to smother him with a pillow while I grind against him.

"Um, so what's that?"

His voice comes out muffled. "Shut up."

EPILOGUE

Evan

Nate said there are never any spectators in the stands, but this is regionals, and people's parents have come out in their nice clothes to watch their kids play tennis under the sun.

Ma and Stacie are sitting next to me in the stands, ready to cheer Nate's team on.

I see Nate's Ma and stepdad walk onto the court, stopping to say something to his coach. His stepdad shakes the guy's hand before saying something to Nate.

Nate smiles and nods. Fuck, he looks good in his fancy-ass, Ivy League tennis clothes. I'm not even embarrassed about having a thing for frat boys anymore—scratch that—having a thing for *a* frat boy. *My* frat boy. He's wearing some off-duty polo with the college tennis logo and a pair of beige chinos with his tennis shoes. He might not be able to play for the rest of this season, but they still expect him to represent the school. He is still a part of this team after all. And he wants to be here to support his friends.

Ben looks up into the stands and waves at us. Stacie waves back with the little Princeton flag Ma bought her at the college store. When we were in there, Stacie got talking to the girl working in the store about athletics programs, and now she's thinking about applying for a hockey scholarship here. I still don't like the idea of her playing that crazy dangerous sport, but if it gets her to Princeton? Yeah, maybe I could get behind it.

I've been brushing up on tennis rules over the past few weeks, watching matches with Nate of his favorite players. I now know the names of at least three famous tennis players —though I'm not promising I can pronounce them all. The doubles stuff is what I'm shakiest on, but I at least understand when the ball goes over the net and when it's completely out.

I met Priestley and Nate's gorgeous ex-girlfriend Mira at a sorority party a few weeks ago (yeah, a fucking sorority party!). I'd expected them to be dicks, but they actually talked to me like I could be a student here. Not the way I expected. Mira didn't even seem that shocked that her ex has a boyfriend now. Like Nate said, she was really fucking nice. She even asked me about my electrician course like I was taking it at the same fancy Ivy League school as these guys. These people live in a different world to the one I'm used to, and that's a good thing. I would rather be a visitor in this world than drag Nate into one where he gets hurt. Even if it takes me a while to figure out how things work here. I'll do it—for him.

Nate sits between his parents and my family, giving my hand a squeeze. His wrist only healed recently, and his cast has been off less than a week. You can still see the skin color difference on that part of his arm. I fucking hate that he got hurt because of me. And I don't want it to affect the rest of his life. No matter how many times he assures me his wrist is gonna heal by next season, I'll never stop beating myself up over it.

Ben and Priestley are playing the double's point together, and even for a novice like myself, I can see they're hot shit.

I lean over and whisper in Nate's ear. "Hey, how come you never told me how good Ben is?"

He shrugs. "Maybe I worried you'd run off with *him*."

"Yeah, right. Because it's your tennis prowess I fell for." I give his leg a squeeze.

After Priestley and Ben take the first set, Stacie leans over and asks if the match is over now. "No, not yet, if they win this set it will be."

Ma grins at me.

"What?"

"Look at you, learning tennis and stuff."

"Psht, whatever."

They take the second set easily and celebrate their win with the team. We all jump up to celebrate. In the heat of the moment, Nate grabs me and kisses me. When we sit down, Stacie pinches me in the hip and I slap her hand away. "Save that violence for the ice, bruiser."

When Ben goes out to play his singles match, my heart is in my throat the entire time.

It must be Nate's nervous energy—rubbing off on me. I barely know Ben, but from the way Nate talks about him—and the fact he helped me out when I'm a total stranger—he's a good guy, and he deserves the win.

When Ben wins the first set, we all jump up to celebrate again. My gaze wanders over to where Nate's ma and stepdad are sitting. They've stood up too and Bryce gives me a little nod while his ma waves to mine but doesn't look at me. I get it, Nate's mom is still mad at me. I'd be mad at me too if I were her.

Ben wins his match and the rest of the team go out onto the court and get a win, advancing them into the next round.

I hang back and let Nate celebrate with his teammates when they all come off the court. Ben comes over to say hi and introduce himself to Stacie and Ma. Stacie kind of blushes when he talks to her and I have to resist the urge to step between them. Even if Ben hadn't told me he's gay and I hadn't witnessed Nate trying to be his wingman—*adorable idiot*—he's not a creep. Nate wouldn't be friends with a creep.

Nate gives Ben a sweaty hug. I'm half expecting Stacie to say *Eww gross,* until I remember she plays sports too. She's probably used to sweaty athletes, hanging around in the girls locker room after hockey games. Anyone who thinks girls can't be as gross as guys has obviously never lived with one.

"Hey," Nate says when he's finished celebrating with his friends. "I'd love you guys to come to dinner with me and my parents, get to know each other. I mean, I know you know my mom, but...." He trails off, rubbing the back of his neck.

"We'd love to, Nate," Ma says.

His shoulders sag with relief. "Great."

I tug him away and ask if he's sure his ma wants *me* to come to dinner.

"Yes. She knows how important you are to me."

I think about telling him that his ma was going out of her way to ignore me all through the match, but I don't want to stress him out so I just smile and nod instead.

When we meet Nate's parents outside the court, Nate's

ma gives mine a hug and Bryce shakes her hand and introduces himself to Stacie as Nate's dad.

Stacie looks at Bryce like she's confused. I have to restrain myself from clamping my hand over her mouth to stop her from saying something stupid like—*Didn't your dad go to get milk and never come back?* But I guess I don't give her enough credit, because she just shakes his hand politely and keeps her mouth shut.

Bryce takes us to some nice restaurant where they serve steak and lobster. It's not so fancy that we look underdressed or feel uncomfortable, but discreetly fancy. Like the food is amazing and there are no kids running around getting snot on everything.

Everyone is talking and enjoying themselves, but I can see Nate's ma eying me every now and then. She's quiet, and when her salad comes, she just picks at it before excusing herself to use the bathroom.

I excuse myself too and wait for her outside the restrooms. I don't know if it's a good idea or not, but I know I need to clear the air. I can't have my boyfriend's ma hating me forever.

When she comes out of the bathroom, I step in beside her and try to push down every instinct telling me to run.

"Hey, Ms. Carter," I start. I think she's gonna ignore me and keep walking. She doesn't stop, but she slows down. "I just wanted you to know, I love Nate."

She stops at that. Takes a deep breath and fixes me in her stare.

"I don't have anything against you, Evan," she says, her shoulders sagging. "I understand you and your family have had a hard time of things since your dad got sick. Joe was a good man, he was always there for me and Nate after his dad walked out. And I know you two have an intense ...

bond. I just worry that you're both trying to hold onto something out of nostalgia."

"It's not nostalgia." I shake my head. "We've changed. And yeah, I was in love with Nate when we were younger, but I fell in love with him all over again the second time we met."

"You're both still so young."

"I know that. But I can promise you something—I'd rather die than do anything to hurt Nate."

"And his wrist?"

I flinch. "Believe me, if I could have stopped that from happening, I would have. But we should both know that Nate's capable of getting hurt or getting into trouble with or without me. We can't wrap him up in cotton wool. He's a grown-ass man. Pardon the curse."

The smallest of smiles twitches on her lips.

"I'm not as bad as people think," I say, actually believing it. Nate must have worn me down. "I don't know why people always assume the worst of me, but I don't want trouble. Never have."

She shrugs. "Trouble just has a way of finding some people."

I snort. "That's the truth."

She looks away, crossing her arms over her chest.

"I love him, I'm not gonna hurt him. Ever."

There's a silence that seems to go on forever before she speaks again. "You took the blame for that stupid stunt back then."

It's not a question so I don't say anything. I have to stop myself from flinching when she reaches her hand toward me before letting it settle on my shoulder and giving it a squeeze. "I believe you."

"Hey, everything okay?" We both turn to find Nate staring at us, wide-eyed.

"Everything's fine, honey," his mom says. I smile and nod my agreement, watching relief wash over his face.

"I just wanted to see if we're ordering dessert."

"Sure, why not?" His ma says with a smile.

When we get back to the table, Stacie's telling Bryce about hockey and he's talking about someone he knows who can put her in touch with the recruitment office of three different Ivy League schools. I smile to myself and shake my head. I'm about to make a joke about Nate's nepotism rubbing off on us when he jumps in.

"She doesn't need your contacts Bryce," he says with a smirk. "By the time she goes to college, mine and Ben's awesome tennis platform might have expanded to other sports. We'll be able to put her in touch with pro coaches and trainers from around the world, and help her apply for scholarships with all the top schools."

Bryce chuckles as he balls his napkin up and tosses it onto the table. "Save the sales pitch for your investors."

Nate laughs, his green eyes with the brown flecks glistening under the ambient lighting. I watch his pretty hands on the table, spreading the dessert menu out. The way he licks his lips as he reads through the list of cakes and ice creams. Something lurches in my chest at the sudden, devastating knowledge that this is the person I've loved all my life. And that nothing in the world will ever change that.

He turns, as if feeling a heat on the side of his face from the intensity of my stare. A blush appearing on his cheeks when he catches me looking.

"What?" he asks. "Do I have something on my face?"

"No," I laugh, taking his hand, threading my fingers

through his. I catch our moms both looking at us with sly smiles.

He leans over and kisses me.

"Eww, gross, get a room!"

We pull apart so I can flick Stacie for ruining the moment.

"A toast," Bryce says.

Nate and I keep our hands entwined as we raise our glasses.

"To Nate."

I'm about to say the toast, when he adds, "And Evan."

Everyone looks at us, their eyes all shiny, big grins on their faces. I don't know whether to groan or cry.

"To us!" I hear Nate say before sipping his champagne. I catch Stacie making a face as she sips her lemonade and my ma leaning in with a smile to say something to Nate's ma as he leans in to kiss me.

THE END

ACKNOWLEDGMENTS

Firstly, thank you for taking the time to read Evan and Nate's story. This story has been kicking around in my head for years. Back when I was still reading a lot of historical and literary fiction and hadn't yet discovered my love of romance—or realized that all my literary/historical fiction had a romance plot.

It is darker than my usual fuzzy romance books, but I felt it was necessary to tell Evan's story with honesty and rawness. It is a story many of us live through—illness and loss of a loved one, feeling isolated and lonely in our surroundings.

One reason why I love the hurt/comfort trope so much is because it is a dream of many to find someone who will help you heal and work through the difficult times in life. I wanted Evan's healing process to be triumphant and for him to enjoy his well-deserved happy ever after.

Thank you to my editor RuthAnn. She always goes above and beyond when editing my messy stories. Fixing my jaunty grammar and patiently teaching me how to get the best out of my writing, while somehow still managing to maintain my individual voice throughout. She has an eye for getting to the heart of my characters' deepest fears and desires and is a genius at finding the best ways to let the reader see them, too. I personally couldn't care less where commas go, but she does, and so that's good!

Thanks to my ARC readers and everyone over on Instagram championing my stories. On days when I need to lift my head off the desk and remind myself that my writing matters, I read your encouraging comments and lovely reviews and it gives me a second wind, helping me march on with the next story.

Finally, thanks to my family and friends who listen to me talk about people who don't exist. Especially Sarah—the best plot-hole spotter in the universe. And my adorable nephew for telling me how proud he is of me all the time. I'm proud of you too, kid! *Also, you shouldn't be reading this!*

Printed in Dunstable, United Kingdom

81275674R00141